The Estate of Mrs. Pearl Whiteman

a novella

The Estate of Mrs. Pearl Whiteman

a novella

Shirley Anne McCormick

Boheme Press
Toronto

Edited by Max Maccari and Andrea Foley

Text and page design by Magpie Media
Typeset in Georgia and Edwardian

Canadian Cataloguing in Publication Data

McCormick, S.A. (Shirley Anne)
The estate of Mrs. Pearl Whiteman

ISBN 1-894498-13-5

I. Title.

PS8575.C686E77 2000 C813'.6 C00-932506-9
PR9199.3.M336E87 2000

Printed and bound in Canada.

Boheme Press
P.O. Box 1017, Station F
Toronto, Ontario, Canada M4Y 2T7
www.bohemeonline.com

Part 1

Bert McCarthy dug his spoon into the steaming bowl of Red River cereal while he scanned the classifieds of the Paisley Herald. He gummed the gooey ball in his mouth a full minute before swallowing. His dentures were hurting his gums lately; he only put them in when he went out in public.

Outside, a warm and cloudless June morning had begun. In spite of the seasonable weather, Bert wore a red flannel shirt with his brown wool pants and suspenders. The sound of a vehicle broke the stillness, and he peered out the grimy kitchen window. A sad-looking green truck without rear fenders turned into his long, straight laneway.

Bert grunted. Henry's boys were coming to finish the haying. Hopefully they would be finished by the end of the week. Bert needed the small income he received from Henry Schwaab for the rent of the fields, yet it didn't stop him from resenting the intrusion of other people using his farm—the land his grandfather had cleared almost a century earlier. He sighed, the weight of close to eighty years heavy upon his tired body.

The small, brick farmhouse was littered with old magazines and yellowed newspapers, and the arms of the solid oak chairs were sticky from the sweat and dirt of farmers' hands from years past. Bert picked up his empty bowl and slowly rose from his chair at the round table. The earwigs scattered as he scuffed across the floor and dropped his bowl in the sink. He'd wash up tomorrow, on Saturday; he always did the dishes on the weekend. Bert had proven them all wrong. Just because he was an old bachelor, his neighbours figured he was a helpless old man. But he could look after himself. It would be four years in September since his sister Angeline had died, leaving him alone on the farm.

Bert leaned on the counter and rubbed his thigh. That left leg still bothered him since the time he fell out of the hay mow about fifteen years before. "Better start taking it easy, Bert," old Doc Bailey had wheezed to him back then. Doc was a heavy pipe smoker; Bert, though, never cared much for smoking, but he did like an occasional shot of rye whiskey. "Must be what's preserved me," he muttered. He picked up the newspaper and flopped into the deep armchair rocker with the colourful patchwork cover that Angeline had made.

Bert swept through the *In Memoriams*, scanned the *Births* and *Thank You's*, and moved on to the *Death* notices. At his age, it was the way he kept in touch with the past and, through his memories, himself. His eyes fell upon a notice that seemed to leap from the page in huge black letters:

At Rest—Pearl Margaret Whiteman, née Varsey.

Bert felt as if he had been punched in the stomach. He tried to slow his rapid breaths, to make them long and slow, like Doctor Lee had instructed him to do when he became excited. For several minutes he breathed, in and out, until his heartbeat steadied. After regaining some control, his shaking hands picked up the paper and he continued to read:

Peacefully, in her home at RR 2, Paisley, on Sunday, June 7, in her 80th year. Beloved sister of Matt, Edward, and Joseph. Loving grandmother of Gerald and his wife, Debra, great-grandmother of Carrie and Lisa. Cremation.

Bert set the paper down across his lap. His whiskered chin trembled and his eyes became wet. "Foolishness!" he grumbled. To be sentimental at this age! He pulled a crumpled and dirty navy blue handkerchief from his hip pocket, and blew his nose with force. Now Pearl was gone. He hadn't even spoken to her since her husband Simon had died, about eight years before. And what was the last thing he had said to her? "My condolences, Pearl." My condolences! Was that all he could find fitting to say? He stifled a low moan and rocked furiously back and forth in the chair.

For most of the past sixty years, Bert had tried to avoid Paisley altogether. And he had been successful, especially since Simon's funeral. He picked up most of his farm supplies in Fagan, a small village about four miles further from the farm than Paisley, even though prices in Fagan were somewhat higher. He even went to the Chinese doctor in Fagan. Angeline did all the food shopping in Paisley, and

Bert often thought it was a blessing that the woman finally got her driver's licence—as stubborn as she was. Now that she was gone, he shopped for groceries in Fagan.

He hadn't always hated Paisley. When he was a boy, his father used to take the children with him in the buggy when he drove into town to buy grain or supplies. They fought over which of them would get to go, and who would ride in the front seat. One strong hand was always needed, usually one of Bert's older brothers. One or two of the younger ones went along for the ride. Bert's mother stayed at home with the rest of the children, except on Sundays when she and her husband drove to mass at St. Boniface Church. The older children would walk behind, while the littlest ones rode in the buggy.

Bert was the third youngest of eight children, and he formed his closest attachments with his little brother, Joseph, and younger sister, Angeline. As they grew older, they barely remembered their oldest siblings: Clarence died at nineteen in the First World War just before its end in 1918, and Mary and Ruth were sent to Toronto to work for a rich lawyer's family as kitchen servants in the early 1920's. They mailed their earnings home and only returned to the farm at Christmas, and perhaps for a week in the summer. To Bert, his family consisted of his parents, the two young ones and himself, his rebellious and carefree brother Donald, and his sister Catherine who worked at the telegraph office in Paisley and only came home on weekends.

All the farm children in that area of rural Ontario, sisters and brothers and neighbours, attended school from the age of six years until entrance class—the eighth grade—if they were lucky, less if they were needed at home on the farm. Very few went on to higher education. Bert kept mostly with his family at school. It wasn't until he was about twelve years old, around 1922, that he began to tire of Angeline and Joseph as playmates. There was another boy in the seventh grade, Matt Varsey, and he and Bert became close friends after the childhood rivalry between them faded. As they approached adolescence, the pair executed acts of extreme annoyance upon the girls, who would appear offended at the time, but giggled amongst themselves afterward.

One morning, as a group of them walked to school, Matt snuck behind Katie Fletcher, snatched her sweater from her arm, and ran ahead with Bert. They hid her sweater high up in the huge pine tree just outside the schoolhouse door. Katie spent a chilly day rubbing her arms, sniffing at the two boys as they teased her. She didn't dare complain to the teacher or they would all get into trouble. After school the boys slipped out ahead of the others, retrieved the sweater, and tormented Katie with it all the way home. When they reached her laneway, Matt threw it at her.

"You boys are going to be sorry!" Katie threatened, as Matt and Bert ran down the road. She clutched the sweater and walked backward toward her home, watching them.

"She's sweet on you, Matt," Bert taunted when they had stopped running, breathless and bent over with their hands on their knees. Matt chuckled; Bert figured he already knew it.

That was the same year Bert noticed, as if for the first time, Pearl Varsey and her long, auburn hair. She was Matt's older sister and was in her last school year, the entrance class. There was talk that she might even go to high school in Paisley if she passed the exam. "You are a very bright child," they had overheard the teacher say to Pearl one day after school.

Bert never pestered Pearl like he did the others. Even speaking to her was difficult, and he blushed whenever she spoke to him. Matt never bothered her either, perhaps in fear of what might happen if she told their parents of his antics at school. Matt teased Bert: "Why do you treat my sister differently from the rest of the girls? Are you sweet on her?"

"Of course not! I have a deep respect for Pearl, that's all."

He dare not admit otherwise to Matt. He knew first-hand what chiding he would endure.

Bert contented himself the rest of that year by observing Pearl: how she laughed, how she scowled over a difficult math problem, how fresh she looked in the morning when the other girls appeared puffy and pale. Pearl was always polite to him and Bert practised being a gentleman by carrying her books home from school. Matt grinned, but restrained himself from commenting when he met with stern glances from Bert.

Pearl passed her entrance exams as expected and attended high school in Paisley the next fall. She rode to town in the buggy on Sunday afternoons with her brother Charles who worked as an apprentice butcher in Paisley. During the week, Pearl stayed at her aunt Matilda's, and on Fridays she and Charles returned home for the weekend.

Bert missed her presence at school but managed to visit the Varsey farm at least once a month to see Matt. He was grateful for that friendship, and it was those times when he might catch a glimpse of Pearl up at the house or in the garden. Occasionally, he even spoke to her.

In spite of his lack of interest in school, Bert managed to do well enough that year to pass his exams. There would be no further education for him; he was greatly needed on the farm. He didn't care much for school anyway; the only good thing it had done for him was give him a chance to meet Pearl.

Educating farm children was a waste of time according to Bert's parents, and he agreed. His future had been arranged from the time he was born. He and his brothers, Donald and Joseph, would run the farm when they came of age, and Bert looked forward to the day. He enjoyed tending the cattle, pigs, and horses, and he liked the feel of his soft bed when he climbed in—his body aching—at the end of a long, hard day. His favourite time of year was the summer harvest, when the families in the area sent their sons from farm to farm to help each other with the threshing of oats, wheat, and barley. They would go to the house for lunch and the women quietly stood aside while the men ate their meals of home-made pork sausage, fried potatoes, and fried green beans. For dessert there was an assortment of pies, usually raspberry, blueberry, red currant, and apple. It made all the hard work worthwhile to a young man.

Bert wished the Varsey's participated in the sharing, but because most of the people in the area were Irish Catholic, Mr. Varsey didn't want to mix with them. It meant that his own sons had to work twice as hard. It meant, too, that Bert didn't get to see Pearl as often in the summer when she was home from school, and he didn't have much time to visit with Matt. Bert wasn't too fond of Mr. Varsey.

His own family was a sanctuary of warmth and humour, making the arduous summer labour less daunting for them all. Bert would stretch out on the couch in the huge kitchen, with his cap perched over his eyes, listening to the music of their laughter as he rested. "Look at the length of you! You're just like your father!" Bert's mother teased Bert in her gentle Irish voice as she flipped the cap off his face. He accepted the compliment with pride. His father was a huge, friendly but stubborn man with a booming voice that could send the children scattering with fear in a moment, and in the next, have them in fits of laughter with his good nature.

Bert and his brothers rarely complained about the hard work, sore muscles, and hands made raw from driving the horses, tilling the soil, and reaping the crops. The twenties brought difficult times for farmers as the market seemingly improved and prices escalated, but not fast enough for the benefits to trickle down to the farming community. Local businesses, however, flourished. But such challenges were not foremost in Bert's mind. His thoughts were of Pearl, and he anticipated each visit to the Varsey farm. He became more brave around her, and spoke to her whenever he could. They grew to be friends, and though she did tend to treat him like one of her younger brothers, he was glad of any attention that she gave him.

When Pearl finished high school in 1927, she moved back home. Bert's visits increased that summer. With the longings of a healthy seventeen-year-old boy, seeing Pearl created a curious mix of pain and pleasure. Her strict Lutheran parents had a grudging acceptance of Bert McCarthy as he was a close friend of Matt's. He helped Matt, Edward, and John with the farm chores when he visited without expecting a meal in return. They were as unaware of his feelings for their daughter as Pearl was herself, and he had no intention of changing that—yet.

It was not often that Mr. and Mrs. Varsey left the farm overnight. But when they received a telegraph message calling them away to Walston when Mrs. Varsey's mother suffered a stroke, they quickly departed. With the old woman's heart condition, they feared she would not survive.

Bert had overheard his sister Catherine remark upon it to the family at the dinner table when she returned from her day's work at the telegraph office. He wasted little time and bicycled to the Varsey farm. Such opportunities were rare.

It was a warm and still August evening and, to his great pleasure, he found Pearl sitting alone on the white wooden porch step in front of the bright, yellow farmhouse. Bert dropped his bike on the grass. Her long, brown-red curls hung around her shoulders, and her cheeks coloured when she saw him. To impress her, he did a handspring toward the step. Pearl laughed.

"Bert, you are a young fool, aren't you?" Her graceful, curved calves and small breasts did not escape his appreciating eyes. He hopped up beside her on the step, panting.

"Want to see some more?" He was a lean young man, brown from the summer labour, and his blonde hair was almost white.

"No thank you! You'll probably take a bad turn and your father will blame us for losing his best hand at harvest time!" Her green eyes crinkled at the corners.

Bert stared at the small, white teeth. He wanted to kiss her pink mouth.

"I heard your grandmother is ill."

"Yes. She hasn't been well for some time. Mother's quite upset. Thank you for asking."

Bert pursed his lips, gave a brusque nod and glanced around the yard. “So, where is everyone?”

“Matt and the boys are down at the barn doing chores, and Charles is over at the Wallace’s. I suppose you’re here to see Matt.”

Bert wondered how much she knew of what he was thinking. “Sure. But I can keep you company for a while, if you like.”

“That would be nice.” They sat quietly, listening to the crickets begin their early evening song. Bert watched her when she looked away, staring at the places where her blue dress clung to her body. Pearl interrupted his thoughts and stood up.

“I have an idea!” Her eyes were full of mischief. “Let’s dance!”

“Dance? I don’t know how to dance!”

She took his hand and pulled him into the house. He was stunned. “Where’s the orchestra?” he joked. His heart pounded with the thought of holding Pearl against him.

She led him through the swinging screen door of the summer kitchen, into the main kitchen, and down a dark hallway into the front parlour. He had never been invited into the Varsey home before.

The ominous faces of Pearl’s ancestors in the portraits that hung on the wall stared down at them with straight, tight lips, adding to the forbidden excitement. There was a gold velvet sofa on the left side of the room and three stiff, black lacquer chairs lined the far wall. Two huge windows with white embroidered lace curtains let in a haunting, golden light from the setting sun. The only sound in the room was the muffled tick-tock from the gingerbread clock that sat on the top of a tall, dark bureau. He was alone in the house with Pearl. Her back was to him, and she made some strange movements with her right arm. Pearl swiftly turned and assumed a dance pose. Music began to play from behind her. Bert jumped back, his eyes bulging. She covered her mouth with her hands and began to laugh.

"What's that?" he said.

"Why it's a gramophone, you ninny!" They studied the tall, oak box that stood in the corner of the room with its lid open.

"I know that! I've heard of them." He watched the record go around. The sound seemed to be coming out of the wooden lattice on the front. He pressed his ear to it.

"It's called *La Favourite*. Charles bought it for mama and papa when he visited Toronto last month," she chirped. Bert was mesmerized and for a moment forgot Pearl, until he felt her delicate touch upon his arm.

"Well?" She took one of his hands.

"Oh, yes," Bert stammered. He took a deep breath and prayed for composure. "May I have this dance, madame?" He gave a deep bow.

"Certainly!" She curtsied, enjoying the play.

Bert took her other hand as Pearl adjusted his arms to place him in a waltzing position, and they began to dance. "It's called *The Vienna Waltz,*" she stated, proud of her worldliness.

"It's very nice."

They looked into each other's eyes as they danced.

Pearl laughed and let go of him when the song finished, and she rushed over and placed another disc on the gramophone. "This is my favourite song!"

Bert watched her hands as she carefully lowered the needle. He was feeling warm, but he didn't want to give any indication that he wanted to stop. It was so deliciously sinful to be in the Varsey home, alone with Pearl.

The music started. It was *The Traitor's Waltz*, Pearl informed him. Bert took her hands and placed them on his shoulders. This time, the music was much slower.

"You're doing very well for a young man who says he doesn't know how to dance," she whispered.

Tiny beads of sweat formed on her forehead. Her eyes darted about the room, and she seemed wary. Bert wondered if perhaps she was worried she might have been too brash, inviting a young man into her home without a chaperone. He hoped not—though he did think she was brazen.

"I have a very good teacher," he replied, reassuring her with his smooth voice, pulling her closer to him as they whirled around the room. They enjoyed their devilment. Opportunities for rebellion were rare in those times of hard work and large families.

When the music finished, the needle scratched at the end of the record. They remained standing in the soft evening light, and Bert looked down into Pearl's face trying to memorize every feature. He wanted to remember this moment—the feel and scent of her—forever. She made no move to back away, and her eyes fluttered and closed. Bert pressed his lips to hers, pulling her warm, strong body against him. She didn't resist. Oh, I am wicked! he thought. Pearl's tranquil eyes looked up at him. He held her hands.

"Pearl, I—"

Suddenly they heard the screen door to the summer kitchen squeak open and slam shut.

"It's Matt!" Pearl pressed her fists together in panic. Matt was in the room within seconds. He was a short, muscular young man with a lock of black hair that had a habit of hanging down on one side of his forehead. He folded his arms across his chest. Bert felt certain his face looked flushed with guilt.

"Hey Bert, what are you doing in here? I saw your bike out front."

"Oh. I just came by to say hello. Sorry about your grandmother. Pearl said you were doing chores. Oh, and she told me about the gramophone, and she was kind enough to show me—"

"Right. I see."

Matt turned away. Bert couldn't tell if he believed him or not. He looked at Pearl, who was speechless. "Well," Matt continued, "I came in for a drink. It's hot out in the barn tonight."

"I'll get it for you," Pearl said quickly, and darted from the room.

"So you like our new gramophone, do you?"

Bert began to wonder if Matt was enjoying the moment, seeing his friend squirm with embarrassment, struggling to regain composure.

"Yes. It's a marvellous machine," Bert said. His pleasure was genuine.

"Why don't you come down to the barn with me, Bert? Doesn't look good, you being alone in the house with my sister. I'm in charge when Charles is away, you know."

"Yes. I understand."

In the kitchen, Pearl had left two glasses of raspberry cordial on the table for them but was nowhere in sight. They finished their drinks, and Bert followed Matt out the door. As they walked to the barn, he turned to look back at the house several times. He didn't see her, but once he thought he saw a lace curtain move upstairs.

Matt acted as if nothing had happened. Bert helped him and his brothers with the chores, trying to pretend that he wasn't thinking of Pearl. But how could he not? He still felt the touch of her fingers upon his arms.

It was dark when they finished working. The boys ambled to the house. "Goodnight, Bert," Matt said as the screen door shut behind him.

Bert was alone in the yard. He picked up his bicycle and looked at the open upstairs window. He noticed the faint outline of someone watching him. It was Pearl.

"Goodnight, Bert," she called down to him in a soft voice.

"Goodnight. I had a terrific evening."

"So did I," she replied. He thought he saw a reflection of light on her teeth as she smiled. "I'll see you again."

"I hope so." You rogue! he thought, pleased with himself.

Pearl let the curtain fall at the window. He sighed and slowly peddled homeward, the music from the gramophone still echoing in his head. He could feel Pearl's softness against him, and the smell of her hair haunted his senses. The bicycle wheels played to him *The Traitor's Waltz*, and he hummed the tune as he rode. Chirping crickets and the crisp coolness of early nightfall enhanced the magic of the evening, and etched onto his consciousness that particular moment when he had never felt more alive. Life had never been more beautiful. As he slept that night he hugged his pillow, reliving that marvellous first kiss.

Bert didn't see Pearl again for several weeks. The intense harvest kept him busy, and Mrs. Varsey's mother died shortly after her stroke. It would have been improper to visit too soon.

In early September, Bert stopped by to see Matt. Nothing was said of the gramophone incident. Pearl did not come out of the house and he began to fret, but before he left she waved goodbye from the upstairs window.

His returned to the Varsey farm two weeks later. This time he very much wanted to speak to her. Again, she wasn't anywhere around the yard. He helped Matt and Edward at the barn with the milking, and when the chores were done they walked to the house where Pearl was waiting on the front porch.

"Hello Bert!" She smiled at him, and he felt the familiar rush of elation and peace she created. Bert wondered how her mere presence could arouse such emotions within him. The four of them walked down the laneway when he left, and they chatted about the weather. She waved to him when he rode away.

His next few visits were like that. While Bert worked with Matt, Pearl would sometimes appear and they would talk for awhile. Then Bert would leave. Nothing much was ever said, and though Bert enjoyed seeing Pearl, he felt desperate to hold her again.

It was almost Christmas when they finally found time to be alone together. He was visiting Matt at the barn and they had just finished the milking when Pearl came through the milk house door bundled in a brown wool coat. She was carrying a small pitcher.

"Hi Bertie. I can't stay very long. Mother sent me down for some cream."

"I'm glad."

He was at a loss for what to say, and scuffed the floor. "Pearl, I've never been able to ask you. I hope you didn't get into any trouble that time we were in the parlour."

"Oh, no. Matt wouldn't say anything."

She stopped smiling and her lips parted. Bert stepped closer. She swallowed hard and seemed nervous.

"I have to go back to the house soon. We're expecting the Minister and mother sent me down for cream."

Bert was pleased that his presence had this effect on her. "So you said."

She fidgeted with the lid before lifting it off the can beside her. She scooped out some cream and it ran down the sides of the pitcher. Pearl set it on the window ledge and looked at Bert. He was overwhelmed by the impact her green eyes had upon him and, powerless over his actions, he pulled her shoulders toward him and kissed her.

"I'd like to see you more often, Pearl."

"You know Father is very strict."

"I know what he's like."

"It's not that he thinks your family's a bad lot; he just doesn't care much for Catholics."

The comment angered him.

"I can't help that he was born a Lutheran!"

He was immediately sorry for losing his temper.

"I mean, none of us can choose what faith we're born into."

"I know. But father would never approve of us."

"Maybe not now. But he will someday. How do *you* feel about us?"

"Well, Mr. McCarthy, I'm very flattered that you find me of interest. I'd like to see you more often as well." His heart felt like it would explode with happiness.

"I'd like to know how we can arrange it."

Pearl was quiet and thoughtful. An impish look crept across her face.

"Matt would never tell Father if we met in secret."

"Are you sure? Matt doesn't know anything, does he?"

She laughed. "Matt told me years ago that you liked me, back when we were in school. We never discuss it. But he knows."

Bert took Pearl's hand. "Well, what about you? What do you think of me?"

"Oh, at first I thought you were a rascal, though I did wonder why you wanted to carry my books all the time. That is, until Matt told me." Bert looked at the floor, embarrassed. "Then I went to school in Paisley and you were often here with Matt and the boys. I just got used to having you around, I guess."

Bert felt rather childish, reminiscent of their school days when Pearl would treat him like an annoying younger brother. His eyes brightened as an idea crossed his mind. "There's a Christmas dance in Paisley next week. Do you think that you and Matt could go and meet me there?"

"I'm sure we could! It's Christmas. I'm certain Father wouldn't think anything of it. What a marvellous idea!"

Bert thought he would burst when he saw the look of delight upon her lovely face. Matt opened the door of the milk house and met their round eyes staring back at him.

"Hey there!" He carried in the heavy milk can. "You two look like you just swallowed canaries."

Pearl squeezed Matt's arm, and Bert felt a momentary tug of jealousy. "Bert just asked if we'd like to go to the Christmas dance next week in Paisley."

"We, you say? He wants to take both you and me, Pearl?" He laughed. "How sweet. Sure! I think that would be a great start to the Christmas season." The three of them proceeded to make plans for the following weekend.

Pearl excused herself. "I had better get back to the house. They'll be wondering what's taking me so long!" Bert's eyes followed every movement until the door closed behind her.

Matt watched him. "I wondered how long it was going to take before you admitted you liked her."

Bert wasn't comfortable with the idea that Matt knew, though he felt proud. "Is it that obvious?"

Matt chuckled and Bert joined him, strangely relieved yet apprehensive of the future. From that moment on, they would all have to be careful of their actions.

Matt's face became serious. It was essential that Bert understood what Mr. Varsey was like, and that they must be cautious. "If he ever finds out," Matt assured him, "It will be a sorry day for the three of us."

The comment confused Bert. "Why? What could he do to us?" The confidence of youth resonated in his voice. That evening, Matt shared his family's shame with his friend.

All of the Varsey children were terrified of their father. Matt told Bert that Mr. Varsey, known as a strict man to his neighbours, was not above striking his children. In fact, he beat the boys with regularity throughout their childhood, for so little as spilling chaff from the cuffs of their pants at harvest time, or playing too loudly in the house. The assaults were fewer as the boys grew older and into strong, young men. Matt recalled a morning a few months back when his oldest brother, Charles, neglected to milk the cows. He had arrived home late from a dance at almost dawn and, not having the energy to do the milking, crawled into bed for a short nap. Instead, he fell into a deep sleep. His father, upon seeing the cows still grazing in the field at half past nine, stormed up the stairs and woke Charles with a buggy whip. From downstairs, the rest of the family heard the wails of Charles begging for him to stop. Mr. Varsey emerged from upstairs with the whip in hand, coolly threw it on the floor, and sat at the table. They heard Charles storm down the stairs and out the front door, and saw him run to the barn with all his might.

Matt's voice was sad, but accepting. "I won't be surprised when Charles disappears. He says he wants to catch a freighter out West to start a new life for himself. Says there's plenty of work out there."

Bert was shocked by these events. "Surely he doesn't hit Pearl!"

"No, and I'm glad for that. We all love her. But she's afraid of him too. She'd do anything to keep him from losing his temper at the rest of us. Usually she and Mother fuss over him, bringing him tea or dessert, anything to distract him when he's upset, to keep him calm. Haven't you ever noticed how jittery she is?"

Bert nodded, remembering the way her eyes darted nervously towards the house whenever she came down to the barn to see them. She was relaxed in his arms, though. She and Matt led such a different life—his own father had never lain a hand on any of the children, despite possessing a loud and boisterous nature. "My father would never hit me," Bert said. He regretted the arrogant words as soon as they left his mouth.

"I guess you're lucky all around," Matt droned. The sense of loss reflected in Matt's face.

"I didn't mean anything by that, Matt." Bert wanted to say more, but was afraid of insulting his friend further.

"I know." Matt hugged him around the shoulder. "You're a good man, Bert. Good for Pearl. Believe me, I won't tell Father about the two of you." With their friendship reinforced, the two young men confirmed the plans for their meeting at the Christmas dance.

Matt and Pearl arrived at the Paisley dance hall without incident, where they met Bert with his sister Angeline, each pair having arrived in their separate buggies. Bert had included Angeline in the secret. She was eager to share the adventure, and could be trusted implicitly—such was the strength of her loyalty to Bert. The four of them acted as if it was a surprise, a chance reunion. They danced, switching partners often, careful not to attract the unnecessary attention of their neighbours. On the way home that night, Angeline and Pearl traded seats in the buggies once they were far enough away from the hall.

Bert cherished the short time he had spent alone with Pearl. They huddled beneath the blanket as he drove the team under the blue moon and across the snowy landscape. Once, he stopped the buggy to kiss her. In the bitter cold, Pearl's chilly nose pressed against his cheek. His lips covered her warm mouth, and flurries of snow blew around them.

When they reached the crossroads of Concession Four and the Sixth Line, Bert stopped the team and helped Pearl down from the buggy. He watched her climb up beside her brother, and as they drove away she waved back at him. "Hurry up and drive," Angeline ranted. "My feet are freezing!"

That night was the first of his many dates with Matt and Pearl. Later on, Matt began to meet Katie Fletcher at the dances. Mr. and Mrs. Varsey approved of Katie and her Lutheran upbringing. She was a nice girl, Bert thought. They let her share their secret.

Bert continued to visit the Varsey farm all winter, into spring, and into another hot summer. Charles, as expected, disappeared one night in early July without a word to the rest of the family. Bert found it strange that they didn't speak about him afterward. Edward was the short brother, two years younger than Bert, with a nondescript face and disturbing, small, close-set eyes. Bert avoided even the most casual conversation with him. "Edward is such a little sneak!" Pearl once hissed. The youngest brother, John, in contrast, was a gentle boy, though he was very simple and constantly needed someone to tend to him and give him direction. Pearl defended him whenever the boys got into a brawl. Next to Matt, he was her favourite.

Bert intentionally missed coming by in the few weeks before and after a dance or party to avoid arousing any suspicion in the Varsey's. On the rare occasion that her parents left the farm, Bert would steal into the house with Pearl while Matt kept the younger boys occupied at the barn. They were never to know. She would play new records for him, one of his favourites being Wilf Carter's *The Wreck of the Ninety-Seven.* Pearl much preferred *The Traitor's Waltz.*

Bert swirled her around the parlour to the music, and they embraced in the unlit room until the sun went down. Bert slipped out of the house before the boys came up from the barn.

With Matt's help, Bert and Pearl spent almost two years seeing each other without the rest of the Varseys' knowledge. Bert's family knew of his feelings for Pearl by this time, and his mother's eyes shone with affection and romance when he came home from visiting her. He had told his parents one evening after a visit to the Varsey farm when he felt he would explode if he didn't share it with them. Bert's father rather enjoyed the fact that his son was seeing Pearl—the daughter of that pompous ass, he scoffed. He found particular amusement in knowing he was aware of it but Mr. Varsey was not.

Bert made plans for the future while he toiled on the farm, dreaming of the time that he and Pearl would marry. They would live here, on the farm where he was born. They would have many sons. Pearl would always be by his side. His longing was intense, and he knew the time was near when it would be too difficult for them to resist temptation and he would make love to her.

On some nights when the moon was full and bright, he looked across the fields from his window toward the east, knowing Pearl's home was over the hill on the next concession, and barely withstood the discomfort. With each visit to the Varsey's it became worse. The mere brush of her body against his raised the passion in him until he wanted to grab her and take her right where they stood. This year he would propose to her. No matter what her father thought or said, Pearl would become his wife.

Bert worked harder than usual in that spring of 1929. Seeding kept him busy and the spring rains made planting difficult. His brother Donald had slipped away on a freight train to Saskatchewan one night as did Charles Varsey and so many of the young men from the area in search of adventure and employment. Donald left Bert, their brother Joseph, and their father to work the farm. Catherine still worked at the telegraph office and that did help somewhat.

The most difficult part was the day young Angeline was sent off to Toronto to work for a doctor's family as a maid. Bert had already lost two older sisters in that manner and they were still living in the city. Ever since they were sent out to work , they no longer made it a routine to visit home. Bert saw the hurt in his parents' eyes as they sent away their last daughter. They couldn't afford to keep all of the children, they'd said. The boys were needed on the farm. "A family does what it must to survive," his father said.

They promised the child they would bring her home again when they could. Bert had to look away as Angeline waved goodbye, her young eyes full of tears. She was his favourite sister and, if he dared admit, his best friend next to Matt and Pearl.

The small McCarthy farmhouse was no longer cramped with brothers and sisters. For the first time, Bert had a bedroom to himself, but his heart ached with loneliness after Angeline left. Even his next visit to the Varsey farm did not ease his sadness as he worked alongside Matt, doing the chores in silence. The younger boys were back in the bush checking on the calves of the outside herd. While Matt was busy milking, Pearl came down to the barn. Her face was glowing.

"Mother and Father have gone to Paisley, Matt," she said, as she cast a warm glance at Bert. "They're going to see some wealthy man about a second mortgage." She explained to Bert that her father was afraid of losing the farm; for the first time, he was surprised to feel a twinge of pity for the man.

"Well I wouldn't be sorry to say goodbye to the farm," Matt called out from behind a Holstein whose soiled tail swished across his face.

Pearl chastised him. "You shouldn't say such things." Bert stared at her and she returned his gaze, holding him with her eyes.

Matt watched them. "Oh go on, you two." His fists pressed rhythmically into the udder of the cow from where he sat, squatting on the small milking stool.

Bert smiled to his friend in appreciation, and he took Pearl's hand as they left the milking parlour. The unusually warm, fragrant, spring evening foreshadowed the hot summer that would soon follow. Pearl smiled at him. Such tenderness shone on her lovely face that his chest ached with longing.

The two of them slowly walked without speaking, hand in hand, to the back of the barn, and drifted inside through the huge wooden doors to the hay mow. The sun was a burning, orange ball above the horizon, and its light shone through the cracks of the barn onto the golden straw. Bert's respirations were deep. He kissed her intensely on the mouth, and her body moulded against him. "I've waited so long to hold you like this," he softly breathed into her ear. He felt her tremble, and looked into her eyes. "Are you cold?"

She smiled, and shyly looked away. "No. I'm not cold." Pearl returned her gaze to him. Her eyes reflected the same aching passion he felt. He raised his eyebrows to question her, wordlessly, and she responded yes, with her damp eyes and open, moist lips. Pearl squeezed his hand.

"Wait here," she said.

He reluctantly let her go and she left him for a moment, but she returned with several burlap feed bags. He watched the movement of her body under the dress she wore as she gently spread the straw to make an even surface, and arranged the sacks on top into a huge rectangle. He dropped to his knees in the middle of the soft bed she had made and pulled her against him. Pearl looked down at him, knowing and accepting what was about to happen, and ran her fingers through his hair.

Bert scooped her off her feet and lay her down. He wanted to memorize the beauty of her auburn hair as it lay strewn on the feed bags, framing the delicate features of her face. He unfastened the buttons on the front of her dress, slipped his hand inside and gently touched her breasts. She gazed at him with her inviting green eyes and pulled him down to her.

They breathed in unison, their lips mere inches apart. Bert kissed her firmly, and she kissed him back with equal fervour. They stroked each other rhythmically as they rolled about on the sacks. Pearl unfastened his trousers. He slid her panties off, and in an instant he was against her, over her, inside of her. Bert felt his body explode as he watched tiny droplets of moisture break upon her upper lip over her delicious, open mouth.

They lay there together afterwards, breathing in unison. He kissed her eyes, her cheeks, her mouth. Pearl was silent and still beside him, her body limp in his arms. Bert admired all of her, profoundly. He wished he could hold her like that forever.

"I love you, Pearl."

She opened her leaden eyelids and smiled. "I hope so. I love you too, Bert McCarthy."

Bert wondered how he could bear to be away from her now. How could he go back to not being with her? He wanted her more than he ever had before. They belonged to each other. "Will you marry me, Pearl?" It had escaped his lips before he realized. The look of surprise upon her face unsettled him.

"Marry you? Oh Bert, Father will never allow it."

"It isn't his decision. We're discussing our lives, not his."

He tried to be gentle as he spoke, to suppress his irritation, though he didn't think he was successful.

"I know that. But it isn't the right time now for Father. He's very worried about losing the farm. And you know how he feels about Catholics."

Her face looked exquisite in the light of the dusk that filtered through the barn boards. Her expression was naive and childlike, but her eyes were knowing, and wanting. I just made love to this beautiful woman, he thought.

"Pearl, all I need to know is that you love me. I want you to be my wife. I want us to have children. I want the whole world to know I love you."

She put her arms around his neck. "I do love you, Bert. And I want to marry you." She kissed his cheek. "But can we wait a year before telling Father? It will give him a chance to get used to the idea. And by then, hopefully, he won't be so worried about the farm—if everything works out with the mortgage."

"A whole year?"

He fought hard not to let his hunger for her make him appear demanding and impatient. "A year. It seems like a very long time."

"Yes, it does. But I know Father. Believe me, it will be better this way. And when we marry, it will be forever."

"Without any doubt." He kissed her on the forehead. "Perhaps a year isn't so long. But we must start getting him used to the idea now, Pearl. Agreed?"

"Agreed," she replied, a trace of apprehension in her voice. He pulled her to him. He had never known such happiness. He would cherish this vision of Pearl, with her hair tousled from their love-making on the feed sacks, for the rest of his life.

They straightened their clothes. Bert gently removed the few pieces of straw that were tangled in her hair. Pearl folded the sacks and replaced them in the bin and they walked toward the barn door, holding hands. Edward was sitting at the top of the ladder that came up from the main floor of the barn, dangling his legs down the hole.

"Edward! What are you doing here?" Pearl demanded in a quivering voice.

"Oh, nothin'. Might be asking you the same thing."

Pearl blushed a deep red. Bert became angry. "How long have you been there?" he demanded.

"Long enough," Edward taunted.

Bert was furious. "Why, I ought to—" He lunged for Edward and grabbed the boy by the scruff of his collar.

"I didn't hear nothin'! Honest! Leave me alone, will you?"

"Well what are you doing then, spying on people!"

"I wasn't spying, honest! I just came up to get a bag of feed for Matt!" Bert let him go. Edward started to cry, then scurried down the stairs. It wasn't long before Matt came up.

"What happened?"

Bert felt ashamed for grabbing Edward so roughly. Pearl sensed his discomfort and touched his arm. "I guess Edward saw us holding hands, and he thought he'd tease us about it," she explained.

"I just sent him up a minute ago for a bag of feed."

"Thank God," Bert muttered.

Matt grinned at his pale friend. "We'll have to keep an eye out for Edward."

Pearl wrung her hands. "What are we going to do?"

"Don't worry about Edward," Matt replied. "I'm going to have a chat with him right now. Make amends. " Matt winked at them before disappearing back down the hole.

Pearl burst into laughter.

Bert huffed, "I don't know how you can laugh at a time like this!"

"I thought you were the one that didn't want it to be a secret anymore!"

He put his arms around her. "We'll start slowly. But your family will have to find out about us sooner or later."

"Yes. We can start this summer."

Bert escorted Pearl to the house and kissed her goodnight. He returned to the barn as Edward was coming out. The boy ran past him to the house, and Bert laughed and went inside.

Matt grinned. "We won't be hearing much out of him."

"Thanks, Matt. Hopefully it won't be a problem for much longer. I've asked Pearl to marry me."

Matt's face was still for a moment, but then he smiled. "Well, congratulations! I figured it was going to happen sooner or later. I mean, how many sleepless nights can a fellow stand?"

"Stop that talk!"

"I wish you luck, friend, I truly do. But you know Father isn't going to make it easy for you. He may forbid it."

Bert laughed. "Forbid it! It's a free country."

"I'm afraid he is something of a cave man in that regard." Bitterness rang in Matt's voice. "It won't be easy, I tell you."

"He doesn't scare me. Anyway, we're going to let him find out about us over the summer, and by next year perhaps he'll accept it. But with or without his blessing, I am going to marry Pearl."

Matt placed his hand on Bert's shoulder and looked into his eyes. "I really hope so."

Bert felt uneasy, but he was determined not to let it ruin his elation.

When he left on his bicycle, he waved to Pearl in the upstairs window. That night in his bed, he relived making love to her. The difficult part now, he figured, would be keeping his hands away from Pearl's lovely body until they married. She had spoiled him now for other women, he chuckled to himself. As he drifted off to sleep, he mumbled, *Good night, my darling Pearl.*

Several weeks passed before he went back to the Varsey farm. He had heard rumours from Catherine that it was possible the Varsey's might indeed lose their farm. It may not be the best time to tell the man about Pearl and himself, Bert thought. But it was more difficult than ever for him to stay away from her. Since the last time he had seen her, he had grown even more eager to marry Pearl.

It was the first Sunday in May. Bert dressed in his best trousers and green tweed jacket, and pulled on his cap. He kissed his mother's cheek on the way out.

"I'm off. Don't hold dinner for me!"

She smiled as she watched her son, now a young man, peddle his bike down the road in the mild, sunny afternoon.

Bert had decided to break tradition. Today, he would visit the Varsey's like a regular visitor—in the middle of the day—rather than at chore time. He would not work like a farm boy tonight; he would go up to their house first instead of straight to the barn.

"It might as well be today that Mr. Varsey learns Bert McCarthy is serious about his daughter," Bert muttered to himself.

He bicycled at a leisurely pace. For all of his bravado he was wary of the confrontation that might occur. Still, he continued, with thoughts of Pearl and her enchanting, green eyes drawing him forward.

When he arrived he noted a shiny black Model A Ford parked by the drive shed. Bert wondered if perhaps he shouldn't have visited without a warning; nevertheless, he had come this far. He leaned his bicycle against the shed. His body was erect as he walked to the imposing yellow house. Bert removed his cap, and as he arrived at the screen door to the summer kitchen, Matt came out onto the porch.

"Hello, Matt."

Matt's face was drawn and pale. His eyes were dark and his upper lip was swollen.

"Oh God, Bert."

"Are you ill? What is it? What's wrong? Where's Pearl, is she alright?" Matt looked like he was going to be sick.

"Yes, yes she's fine. What are you doing here now?"

Bert was puzzled. "I thought it was time. What on earth is the matter?"

"Bert, you should go now. I'll walk with you."

"But where's Pearl?"

Bert panicked.

What if she was pregnant? A sinking feeling came over him. No, she couldn't be. That was only a few weeks ago.

"She's not going to have a baby, is she?"

Matt stared at him. "Oh Bert, you didn't!"

Bert was embarrassed. "Never mind that now."

"Well, she's not pregnant as far as I know. That's not it. Please, Bert, let's go. I'll explain everything."

Bert felt sick with worry that something had happened to Pearl.

"I'm not leaving until I know she's alright!" He whisked past Matt through the screen door and knocked at the kitchen door. Mr. Varsey opened it. He was a tall, thin but muscular man with a thick handlebar moustache and small eyes. I see where Edward gets his looks, Bert thought sourly. Behind him, Pearl and her mother sat at the table. Bert recognized Simon Whiteman from the lumber mill casually reclined in an armchair by the window. Pearl's eyes were red and puffy, and she looked up at Bert. He wanted to run past Mr. Varsey and go to her.

"What is it?" Mr. Varsey barked.

"I would like to see Pearl."

"I'm afraid she can't speak to you. We're rather busy at the moment."

Bert noticed Simon Whiteman's smug expression in the background. His skin bristled, and he felt Matt pulling at his sleeve.

"Come on, Bert," he pleaded.

"Yes. Do take your young friend away," Mr. Varsey said, narrowing his eyes.

Bert watched Pearl's face until the door closed in his face. He reached to open it but Matt grabbed his arm, and they wrestled for a moment. Bert flung him to the floor.

It was then he noticed Matt's neck had a huge purple bruise below his right ear. Bert helped him up.

"I'm sorry, Matt."

"It's alright. Now please, let's just get out of here. I'll explain."

Bert picked up his cap and dusted off his pants. He took his bicycle and they walked down the laneway. He looked back at the house for a sign from Pearl, but she didn't come to any of the windows. The world did not make sense to him. The only constant was the evil in Mr. Varsey. It radiated from his eyes.

Bert was stunned by what Matt told him. He walked along in a daze, pushing his bike. They stopped at the schoolhouse and sat beneath the huge pine tree. Matt hung his head, and Bert wept.

Apparently a few weeks before, on the last night that Bert and Pearl had seen each other, the Varseys had been invited to dinner in Paisley by Simon Whiteman. He was about thirty-five and considered quite handsome. It was said he had always been a bachelor and a lady's man, with his brown skin and dark hair and eyes. Simon was the only child of Harold Whiteman, owner of the lumber mill in Paisley who had died about five years earlier. Since its beginning in 1890, the mill was an institution in the county. Next to farming, it served as the main source of economy in the area.

Whiteman was a Lutheran who attended the same church as the Varsey's, and it was there he first became attracted to Pearl's lovely young form. Later when she attended school in Paisley, he saw her daily as she walked to and from her aunt Matilda's. Over the past two years he was content to see her at service on Sunday mornings, waiting for an appropriate time to approach Mr. Varsey and for Pearl to be of a respectable age to marry. He had heard of the Varseys' financial difficulties and saw a way to resolve their financial woes, as well as achieve some of his own goals.

Whiteman was a shrewd businessman. He offered a second mortgage on the Varsey farm as a gift in return for one third ownership of it, but on one condition—that Pearl be permitted to marry him. In addition, there would be a position at the mill for Matt.

Varsey had no qualms with the arrangement. Mrs. Varsey would never dare to raise a voice against her husband, so what she thought was of no consequence. Having a businessman in the family would be good insurance that the Varsey farm would never be sold, Mr. Varsey had reasoned. Besides, Pearl was now twenty years old, and not getting any younger.

Bert was distraught. While he had been making love to Pearl, her father was making plans to sell her to a wealthy man.

"But Matt, what about Pearl's wishes? What about me?"

"I tried to tell him."

Bert winced at the swollen, loyal eyes of his friend. "He did that to you?" Matt nodded. "I'm sorry you had to take that on my account."

"And Pearl's."

Blood rushed into Bert's neck. "Did he hurt her?"

"It's alright, Bert. He only slapped her once, then he came back to me."

"The bastard!" Bert kicked and pounded the door of the schoolhouse.

"I know. He's a swine. I'm getting out of that house."

"Where are you going?"

"I told you. I'm taking the job at the mill with Whiteman."

"You can't be serious. How could you? Pearl isn't going to marry him!"

"Yes, I'm afraid she is."

Bert was frantic. "No, I tell you! I'll take her away if I have to!"

"If you do that, you'll never be able to live around here and work on your precious farm." His acid comment stung Bert. "I'm sorry, friend. I shouldn't have said that. But in all honesty, Pearl could never defy Father and live just a few miles away from him as well. You don't understand, do you? You've never had to deal with anything like this in your own family."

"I know enough to realize that a man's life is his own. I know Pearl loves me. And she'll marry me, you'll see!"

"You are very naive." Defeat radiated in Matt's words. "I'm not saying this to hurt you. But for God's sake, Bert, your own parents shipped out three of your sisters to make money. So don't act high and mighty with me! Everyone's having trouble keeping their farms and being fed these days. This is something Pearl's doing to help the family. I kind of understand the unselfishness of it, like Father was saying."

Bert felt nauseous.

"She hasn't done anything yet, and she won't marry Whiteman if I can help it! You're some friend, Matt Varsey."

"I am your friend, Bert. But I have to consider my future as well."

"That's what it all comes down to, doesn't it? What's good for you. You don't give a damn about Pearl."

"That's a lie!" Matt leapt to his feet, and the two of them stood with their fists clenched, staring at each other. Matt dropped his hands slowly and shook his head. "I don't want to fight you, Bert. But I will if I have to."

Bert dropped his fists. Matt sat down and took a deep breath. He continued. "If I get a job at the mill I can leave that wretched farm. I'm not like you; I hate it. I work from the time the sun rises until it sets, every day, and all bloody summer long. And the old man pounds on me whenever he gets worried about losing the damn farm. Well, let it go I say! I don't care. When I get a job at the mill, I can start a life away from this godforsaken place."

"I understand, Matt. Really. But you know he won't hire you unless he gets your sister in trade, like she was chattel! I won't let it happen as God is my witness!"

Matt stared at the ground as if he was no longer listening.

Bert felt betrayed. He picked up the bike and left Matt sitting at the base of the tree. As far as he was concerned, their friendship was over.

Part 2

Fuelled by fury, Bert rode his bicycle home as fast as he could. He arrived in a sweat, and rode past the house and barn to the back gate. He hoped his family didn't see him come in the driveway. With his state of mind, he could not speak to anyone. They would not be able to understand the wickedness of Mr. Varsey any more than Bert could. He leaned his bicycle against the post, tossed off his beloved tweed jacket and ran to the back of the farm, delirious in anger and disbelief. He sat in the long grass beside a fallen log, and watched the cattle munching. Hours passed like minutes, and after the night fell he stumbled back to the house and crept up to his bed.

That night, Bert was unable to sleep. The next day, he couldn't eat. After morning chores, he worked in the drive shed, repairing the plough and getting the thresher ready for the upcoming season. He milked the cows again in the barn at night, not speaking to his brother Joseph, responding to his questions with only a grunt or a nod. He didn't come into the house until after the sun had gone down.

Bert sat at the kitchen window and stared into the blackness. His mother rubbed his shoulders. "What happened, dear? Why don't you talk to us?"

He shook his head and patted her hand. If he tried to speak he might cry. Bert didn't think he could endure that humiliation in addition to everything else.

"Let the boy be," his father said. He patted the sofa beside him, beckoning his wife. He understood his son—sometimes a man needs silence, needs to be alone. Bert climbed the stairs to bed.

His heart beat strongly, making sleep impossible. Bert's mind reeled with thoughts. He relived the events of the previous day, over and over in his mind. He knew he had to see Pearl, to talk to her, bring some sanity back into their lives. When they saw each other again, when he had a chance to hold her, he was sure everything would be alright. They could beat this. He pondered the possibility that Matt might be right, that Pearl might not want to live in the same community as her family. If they had to, he decided, they would run away somewhere and make their own life together. Then maybe someday, after things settled down, they could come home again.

He felt a stab of regret and sadness at the thought of leaving his home. Perhaps Joseph would marry and raise a family in this house before they came back, and he and Pearl wouldn't be able to live at the farm. He pushed the thought from his mind and forced sleep upon himself. He decided that the next night, once everyone had gone to bed, he would sneak over to the Varsey farm.

Bert awoke the next morning to the sound of rain pelting against his window. He managed to force a piece of sausage down, but his appetite was gone. The day dragged on, and he kept himself busy with chores. The evening was drizzly and grey. He waited until almost dark before he cycled to the Varsey's, hid his bicycle by the trees at the end of the lane, and walked up the driveway to the house.

The sound of voices emanated from the kitchen. Bert crouched beneath Pearl's window on the second floor and saw a light burning inside. He picked up some small stones and threw them lightly, one by one, against the glass. A short while later Pearl looked out and upon seeing him she opened the window.

"Pearl! I've got to see you," he called in a whisper from behind a small bush.

"Everyone is still awake. I can't come down until they go to bed."

"I'll wait." Pearl closed the curtain.

It was almost two hours before the last lamp went out in the house. Bert sat huddled in the drizzling rain, his clothing drenched. At last, Pearl crept out through the front door. Together they hurried to the milk house at the barn. Once inside, Pearl lit the coal oil lamp. "Bert! You're soaking wet!" she cried. Bert saw the sadness in her eyes.

"Never mind that. What's going on here? Matt told me some of it; please tell me it isn't true."

Pearl turned away from him and covered her face with her hands.

"Look at me," he ordered, and grabbed her arm. "Can't you see that I'm out of my mind with worry? What's happening?" She faced him, and her eyes were wet with tears. He began to feel he was caught in a hopeless situation.

"Oh, Bert. Papa will lose everything unless I marry Simon Whiteman. He's my father, Bert. I must do as he says."

He considered for the first time that perhaps she might not marry him. “No, Pearl! You don’t have to listen to him, not when your whole life is at stake. He can’t force you to marry the man!” He lifted her chin to him and noticed the left side of her face and mouth were swollen. “Did he do this to you?”

“He only hit me once, when I told him about us. He will never forgive Matt and me for deceiving him, unless I make it right. He told us, *children who deceive their fathers are destined for hell.*”

“Oh, Pearl.” He pulled her to his chest and held her close to him. “And what does he say about a father who beats his children? That can’t be right.”

“I don’t know what’s right or wrong anymore!” She pushed away from him and sat on a milk can. “He says Simon Whiteman is a good man—”

“What are you saying? How can you even speak of another man?”

Pearl’s face had taken on a glazed expression, and she replied in a wooden voice. “I can’t go against my father. *Honour thy father and thy mother—*”

“Please Pearl, I’m begging you. Don’t give up so soon! Marry me. We’ll go live at our farm.”

She looked in his direction, but not at him. “I couldn’t do that. My family would never speak to me again! I couldn’t live through that. Why, the entire Lutheran congregation would consider me an outcast. And what would that do to our children?”

“Damn the congregation!” He composed himself before making his last suggestion. “We can run away. We can go West. I’ll get a job on the wheat farms this summer; there’s still work. Then, in a few years we can come home again.”

"And what would we do after the summer? There aren't many jobs to be had over the winter. Where would we live? We could starve to death and no one would care. No one would know us. What if we had a child with us?"

"We'll manage," he replied weakly. He felt as if a battle had been lost.

Pearl's glum face looked up at him. "Bert, I can't leave. We'll lose the farm, don't you see? We have no money! We'll be going to the poorhouse and we won't have a home anymore. I can't do that to my parents! The banks won't lend Father any more money. Why, another bank in Walston closed last month because so many farmers couldn't repay their debts. This is the last chance for my family. Simon Whiteman's the only one willing to give us the money to keep the farm, and it's a generous gift! How can I walk away from them now? They are the people that gave me life!"

"But they're selling you! I thought you were mine."

She looked at him. He saw the love in her eyes, but they reflected helplessness. Just a few weeks before, life was full of hope, with dreams at their fingertips ready to be grasped. Promise had abandoned them.

Bert shook his head and ran his hands through his wet hair. "How could our lives have changed so suddenly?"

Pearl stared at the reflection of light in the window. "We can't do anything about this, Bert." He stood in front of her as she sat, and she leaned her cheek against his chest, crying softly. He patted her auburn hair and tightly squeezed his eyes shut.

"It will happen very soon. Papa's deadline for the payment is the first of next month. Whiteman wants the marriage before then."

"How could he do such an unspeakable thing as this?" His confidence had left him. He felt her warm breath upon his chest and understood the passion that must have consumed Simon Whiteman.

Bert pulled away from her, his vision blurred by tears. "I must go now." He leaned down and kissed her moist cheek. From the doorway, without looking at her, he spoke. "If you change your mind, please come to the farm. I love you Pearl."

He left the milk house and slowly walked toward the laneway. Pearl watched him from the barn. "It's not up to me," she croaked.

He kept walking. He thought he heard her calling him through the mist but he didn't look back.

Bert stumbled in the grey fog, past the house, and out the lane. He left his bicycle and walked home in a daze in the cold drizzle, stopping along the way to sit and catch his breath. His throat ached and he sobbed openly, with no one but the cattle in the fields to hear. Bert lay in the cool, wet grass for a long while. It was almost dawn when he reached home. He collapsed in the yard.

"Pneumonia!" Bert's mother scurried behind Doctor Harding as they left Bert's bedside.

"Yes," the doctor growled, his spectacles sliding down his huge nose. "He should have known better than to be out in that cold rain. Keep him in bed for at least a week or two or you'll be losing him!"

Bert lapsed in and out of sleep, coughing and wheezing. He mumbled a few words before drifting off to sleep again.

It was a full week and four days before he was lucid enough to carry on a conversation. His mother was with him.

"Ma?" he choked.

"Yes, Bert, my boy. How are you feeling?"

Her warm smile comforted him, and she held his hand.

"Poorly."

"We know, Bert," her voice gently droned. "We know about Pearl, too, son." She admired him with the loving gaze of a mother who cannot bear to see her child in pain. "Her brother Edward found your bicycle a few days ago. He rode it over here before the wedding."

Bert's throat tightened. "Wedding?" He wished he had died.

"Yes, love. She was married on the weekend."

"I didn't think she would do it. I really believed she loved me." His mother stroked his cheek as he wept.

That evening Bert heard his parents talking in the kitchen, and feeling well enough to get out of bed he started down the stairs to join them. He heard his mother speaking: "I wanted to tell him, 'Yes, son, I'm sure she loves you'. But Pearl Varsey is another man's wife now, and it wouldn't be proper. I despise that Simon Whiteman for what he's done. What a lecherous manner to be getting a wife!"

His father said something that Bert couldn't make out. His mother continued.

"Yes, I can understand even that demon Varsey's fear of losing his farm. To think that we've sent three of our own babies away to work for strangers! It's a wonder any of us sleep at night." Bert heard a quiver in her voice. "My, these are hard times for us all. In many ways."

His chest was pounding. Bert climbed back up the stairs and crawled into bed.

It was several weeks before he felt he had enough energy to work. Gradually, he regained his strength and began to take an interest in the farm. He threw himself into his labours, filling his mind with thoughts on how to improve the yields of corn and oats, deciding which cattle should be culled from the herd, and how many pigs should be slaughtered for winter.

Bert heard that Pearl and Simon had moved into the Whiteman family home next to the mill in Paisley, and that Matt had taken a room with them. Bert avoided going to town. He couldn't bear it if he ever saw Pearl with her husband. His father understood, and took Joseph with him instead to help with the feed and supplies.

The economy took a severe blow that fall. The stock market crashed on Black Thursday, October 24, 1929. By the following week the country was in an uproar as people sold their stocks in panic. Many lost their savings, and some took their own lives after losing everything they owned. Farmers were already used to the hard times of the twenties, though the crash made things even more difficult for them. Many of the store owners couldn't afford to buy their produce and livestock, and those who could didn't want to pay a high enough price. Several businesses closed, but Simon Whiteman's lumber business held on. He had spent a good portion of his capital when he bought the Varsey farm; he also owned a couple of other farms in the area, leaving little tied up in stocks.

Bert's family didn't lose much since they didn't have a great deal of money even before the Crash. They survived through self-sufficiency: supplying their own meat, eggs, milk and poultry, and stocking the cold storage with potatoes, turnip, cabbage, pumpkin, cucumbers, and carrots.

But they did need to buy sugar and flour, and other things they could not make on their own. Mrs. McCarthy dried apples on top of the cooking stoves until they were feather weight, then sold them for a few cents a pound to the general store in town. His mother often grimaced upon her return, saying the owner criticized the quality of her apples, then offered her a lower price.

"I'm sure he sells them as top quality, though!" she complained.

That, and the apple butter she made—a blend of apple and pumpkin—earned a small income, enough to buy the supplies needed for pickling and for preserving raspberries, peaches, and plums. The McCarthy's were not rich, but they certainly would not starve.

Just past the New Year, Catherine came home for a few days vacation from the telegraph office in Paisley with an announcement that shook the family. She told them at dinner that Pearl had given birth to a baby boy. Catherine didn't see the colour drain from Bert's face, nor her mother's stern glance, silently pleading with her to stop.

"Apparently Pearl had quite a difficult time. Doc Harding told her she might not be able to have any more children. I saw Pearl and the child this week, and she looks a bit thin. The baby's adorable, I tell you."

Bert left the table while Catherine carried on with her story. He didn't want them to see—or feel—his pain. His mother's eyes followed him out the door, and he heard her scold Catherine. "Hush up with your gossip! Can't you see how it's upsetting your brother?"

Bert felt the familiar nausea he awoke with every morning since he'd heard that Pearl had married Simon Whiteman. And now she had a child whom she would raise with the wealthy scoundrel. Bert didn't think he could ever feel as much torment and disappointment as he did that moment. All he could do, the only thing within his power, was to steel himself against it. There was no denying now that Pearl was no longer his.

The 1930's brought an end to many family farms but the McCarthy's kept theirs, as did the Varsey's. Bert thought he must have been a very naive young man to ever have believed he could have run away with Pearl and survive. He immersed himself in his labours on the farm. That, at least, was something he could depend on—the work was never-ending.

In 1933, a huge storm passed through the county. Some said it was a tornado. The McCarthy's hid in the basement when hail the size of golf balls banged against the window and the sky turned to a dark green. From below, they heard the crash of glass. After the heavy winds subsided, they climbed the stairs to find a window had been broken by the hail but the barn was intact. The cattle by the barn and in the back fields were skittish, but otherwise healthy. Part of the implement shed was torn off; it would need repair.

When the large load of lumber was ready at the mill for pick up, Mr. McCarthy made it very clear that he would need both of his sons with him. A stern and silent Bert drove into Paisley with him and Joseph.

The two brothers waited outside until their father came out of the mill with Matt Varsey. Matt smiled. "Hello Bert!" He was a bit too cheerful, he thought. "Haven't seen you in a long time."

Bert looked through him. He jumped down from the wagon and helped load the wood in the back. Matt frowned and gave a slight shrug, and Joseph patted him on the shoulder. The four of them worked together in silence. Bert heard a soft voice behind them amidst the din of sawing wood.

"Matt!" Bert turned around, and at the door of the mill stood Pearl. A small, fair-haired boy clung to her knees. She was wearing a pale yellow dress with puffed sleeves, and her hair was bobbed short around her neck. She recognized him, and her mouth fell open.

Matt said to Bert, "Come on. I want you to meet my nephew."

Bert ambled in a daze toward her and looked into her green eyes that seemed to plead to him. For what? he wondered. Matt crouched down to the small figure.

"Bert, this is Peter."

Bert's eyes left Pearl and he looked down at the child. His blonde hair was almost white from the sun, much like his own, and his eyes crinkled as he grinned up at the stranger. He buried his head into his mother's knees and she laughed and stroked his head.

Hearing her laughter was magic for Bert. He smiled at the child. "Hello, Peter. You're a handsome little fellow." Someone from inside the mill called for Matt, and he disappeared through the doorway. Bert's eyes explored Pearl's captivating face.

"Hello, Pearl." The yearning that he thought was buried deep inside him rose to the surface.

Her lips pursed as she tried to stifle her words. "Bert—"

"My God, you're lovely," he whispered. He missed her, not realizing how much until she stood before him. The child tugged on Pearl's skirt, focused on the men loading the boards behind them.

"Don't, Bert, please." She held the boy's small arms against her legs, and took a deep breath as if to fortify herself. "For so long I've wanted to tell you I'm sorry."

"There's nothing to say now, Pearl. It's past."

Her lips quivered and he thought he couldn't stand to be there any longer. He ruffled the child's hair and looked into her sad but beautiful face. Before he could stop himself, he took her by the shoulders and kissed her warmly and quickly on the mouth. He let go of her and his eyes became wet. As he turned to leave, a sharp voice called out.

"McCarthy!" Simon Whiteman strode toward him, his face puffing and red. "Keep your filthy farmer hands off of my wife!" His teeth were clenched. Simon grabbed Pearl's arm roughly and she winced.

"Simon!" she squealed. The little boy clutched his mother and looked up at the stranger with fear in his eyes.

"Don't you ever show your face around my mill again, or it'll be a sorry day for you!" Simon stomped off, dragging Pearl by the arm. Peter ran behind them.

She looked back at Bert in alarm and almost tripped. He wanted to run to her and punch Whiteman in the mouth before taking her and the boy away with him. But she was Simon's wife.

"What on earth ever possessed you to do a thing like that!" his father screeched at him on the drive home. "As if times weren't bad enough! If I can't get my lumber from Whiteman I'll have to go clear over to Harrisburg to get it, and it'll take me all day! So help me . . ." he trailed off. Bert was silent. He had had enough confrontations for one day. "By God, if you can't control yourself around that woman you're no better than some raving lunatic!" His father was more furious with him than he had ever seen.

When they arrived home and unloaded the lumber, his father was still cursing and grumbling. All Bert could think of was Pearl: her warm mouth, the handsome child—and Simon Whiteman. He felt coldly certain that he could kill the man with his bare hands if he ever saw him hurt Pearl or the child. That night, Bert dreamt that he made love to her on a huge, feather mattress, and Simon came into the room, saw them and flew into a rage. Bert beat his fists into Simon's belly and face and threw his body out the window, and he and Pearl laughed and laughed.

He woke up in a cold sweat. I must be going mad, he thought. Bert decided—no matter what—he would never go to Paisley again.

The hard times of the thirties finally passed after the new prime minister was elected in 1935. After leading the Opposition for five years, the Liberal, William Lyon Mackenzie King would help the people get their lives back in order. But then came the Second World War in 1939 which seemed to drag on forever. Joseph enlisted in 1944 after he turned thirty. He was a healthy and strong young man who wanted to help put an end to Hitler's rampage. On the day he left, he sang the popular tune, *Doin' What Comes Naturally*, in the comical way he always had as Bert drove him to the station. Joseph was killed four months after he enlisted.

The war ended shortly thereafter. Bert's father suffered a severe stroke in the fall that paralyzed his left side, and

Angeline came home from Toronto to help her mother care for him. She had never married. Now with Joseph gone, only Bert remained at home. Bert was elated that his favourite sister moved back home, and felt some of his youthful joy return. Catherine married Frank Comben, owner of the General Store in Paisley, an old widower with two grown sons. Bert only saw Catherine when she came home to the farm. Their older sisters never came home. The only contact with the family occurred through Christmas cards and the odd letter.

1946 was a difficult one for Bert. His father suffered another stroke and, after a brief time of being bed-ridden—something he could never endure—passed away. Bert missed the companionship and laughter of his father and Joseph, as well as their helpful hands. He ran the farm alone. Angeline helped by feeding the livestock and looking after the gardening and the chickens. Their mother was never quite the same lively woman after her husband died; she became withdrawn, consumed by her knitting.

Hydro came through the county in 1948, and the McCarthy farm was the first on the concession to be hooked up. They had a telephone installed shortly afterward, and indoor plumbing came two years later. Bert missed neither the coal oil lamps nor the wind that blew from below when he used to sit in the draughty outhouse on a cold winter day. And, like many of their neighbours in the early fifties, they bought their first motor vehicle—a half-ton Ford truck. Bert loved the freedom it offered, and the speed, so much faster than the horse and buggy. Angeline was a willing passenger, having been used to the city and its buses, but she refused to get behind the wheel. It took years before Bert convinced her to take up driving.

The family didn't hear much of the Varsey's anymore, except what Catherine told them when she came over from Paisley.

On her last visit they learned that, apparently, young John Varsey never did develop properly. The family couldn't look after him anymore and since he couldn't care for himself, they sent him to a special home in Guelph.

Matt had married Katie Fletcher in 1935 and they never had a family, though Katie told Catherine she wanted to have children. Matt spent a lot of time with Pearl's boy. Edward, still a bachelor, looked after the Varsey farm and Mrs. Varsey since Mr. Varsey died in 1948, supposedly of cancer. He withered away before dying a slow and agonizing death. Doc Harding said his abdomen was an open sore and there was nothing they could do for him but bathe the wound. When Bert heard the news he felt no revenge or anger or pity—just acceptance, as if it were expected: a fitting end to an evil life.

Pearl's son, Peter Whiteman, fell for a young girl, Susan Butz, and got her into trouble. She was only sixteen and still in school. Peter was just nineteen himself. Her parents disowned her so Pearl and Simon took her in. Pearl was quite upset about it, and apparently Simon was very angry. But Peter claimed he loved the girl. They married in 1949, and Peter worked at the mill to learn the business. They named the baby boy Gerald.

Bert found all the talk of the Varsey's unsettling, bringing his memories to the forefront of his thoughts. He had worked hard to keep them in the past. But peace of mind was not to be. One crisp, November day, upon her return from shopping in Paisley, Angeline entered the house looking very pale. Bert asked what was wrong.

"I heard some distressing news when I was in town." He immediately thought of Pearl. Angeline's voice wavered. "There was a bad accident at the mill."

Bert hoped for Simon, then felt ashamed.

"Matt was working at the saws and one of the belts became stuck. He tried to pull it loose and it started up again, catching him by the sleeve. Young Peter came in and saw his uncle with his fingers cut off, and his hand jammed between the frame and the blade. He tried to pull Matt away."

She started to weep. "Peter lost his balance after he pulled Matt out, and he fell into the blade. His arm was cut off. There was blood everywhere, they said. They couldn't stop the bleeding. By the time they got him to the doctor, he was dead. What a horrible tragedy!"

She cried openly. Bert put his arm around his sister and thought of the small, blonde boy that clutched his mother's knees years before.

It was a huge funeral. Nearly everyone in town attended, including those people who had scoffed when young Peter and his wife were married. Breaking his promise to himself, Bert once again went to Paisley.

He found a spot in a pew at the back of the church. Simon sat stone-faced in the front row beside Pearl, who sat bent with her face in her hands. She moaned throughout the service. The young widow, Susan, was very still beside her mother-in-law. Edward sat behind them. Bert didn't see Matt.

After the rites, the pall bearers, none of whom Bert recognized, slowly wheeled the gilded casket from the church. Simon helped Pearl, weak from sorrow, to her feet. She said something to him and then he left with Susan. Edward stayed behind and led Pearl out of the church after everyone had left. Bert waited for them at the exit.

Edward smiled sadly at him while they stood in silence. "I'll bring the car around, Pearl," he said to his sister. He nodded to Bert before leaving the two of them alone on the church steps. She blinked her eyes.

Bert wasn't sure if she was aware of his presence or not. He swallowed and fought the pain in his throat. "Pearl, I'm so sorry."

"So am I," she croaked. She looked old and tired, though barely forty. "He was a good boy, my Peter."

Bert remembered the child's smile, the only time they had seen each other—the boy looking up at a stranger. "I'm sure he was."

"This wasn't supposed to happen, Bertie."

She hadn't called him that since they were children in school. "No, it shouldn't have." He wanted to comfort her, to hold her, and let her cry on his shoulder.

"He was trying to save Matt, did you know that?"

"Yes, we heard about it."

"Heard about it!" she spat. The anger in her voice shocked Bert.

Edward drove up in a green Nash. Pearl turned to Bert with red-rimmed eyes and tensed her lips. In a soft voice she said, "He was your son, Bert."

Bert was speechless. He had wondered about it all these years. Now he knew. He had a son. Bert touched her arm, and she stiffened. "Simon doesn't know. He must never know," she whispered.

"I understand." He knew it wasn't the right time, but he heard himself say, "I love you, Pearl."

Her eyes filled with tears and she touched his arm as she looked at him. "I've always counted on it," she said, and turned and stepped down the stairs. Edward helped her into the car. He gave Bert a curious glance before driving away. Pearl didn't look up again.

Bert stood there for a long while before leaving the church. As he drove through the town, he looked at the shops and houses like he was a tourist on vacation. He vowed that he would ever come back again. Paisley held nothing but sadness for him.

That evening, in the bitter winds of late fall, he walked the fields of his farm envisioning his family that never was, thinking of the son he had lost and never known. And he had a grandson, Gerald, whom he had never seen. Once he had tormented himself to the point he could no longer stand the pain, he dropped to the ground on his knees and cried.

Through to the following spring, Catherine kept the McCarthy family informed of all the news about the Varsey's and the Whiteman's.

The young widow, Susan, had run off to Montréal without the baby. Apparently she was afraid she couldn't raise the child alone without his father. She had left a note, and the baby with Pearl and Simon. Pearl was raising Gerald like he was her own.

After the accident, Matt Varsey couldn't return to work at the mill. The rumour was he couldn't stand the guilt. He and Katie moved to Walston and Matt took a job at the brick factory. Pearl and Simon couldn't bear the sight of the lumber mill any longer so they sold it to the owner of the Harrisburg mill. They moved back to the Varsey farm to live with Edward and Pearl's mother who wasn't doing very well at the time. Pearl looked after both her and the child. Mrs. Varsey passed away a few short weeks after they had moved back.

Catherine didn't hear much more about the Varsey's once they had all left Paisley. Bert and Pearl lived their separate lives as strangers, each on their own farms mere concessions away, and never crossing paths. It would be almost fifteen years before Bert would see her again. It was in Fagan, 1967—Canada's Centennial.

The town was in celebration and the summer brought endless parties, fairs, and dances for the public. Angeline had wanted a night out on the town for years. She had pestered Bert all spring to take her to the dance. After years of caring for the elderly Mrs. McCarthy, who was becoming more senile and difficult to live with, Angeline needed a break. Bert admitted she deserved a night out so they asked a neighbour to stay with their mother.

On the Saturday night of the dance, after he finished the chores and took a bath, Bert pulled on a colourful blue and green summer shirt and a pair of beige, cotton pants. He slapped on some aftershave. He and Angeline drove to Fagan in high spirits.

Old-time country music was blaring from the town square when they arrived. They left the old truck in the parking lot a block from the street dance. A few teenagers howled, drinking beer from the case in the back of their open pick-up truck. Bert chuckled.

Angeline huffed, "I don't find their impudent behaviour amusing!"

"I thought you wanted a night out," he teased. "Or did you think we were going to a tea party?"

"Don't be smart with me, Bert." She poked him in the ribs. "I just better find someone to dance with me, or you'll be in trouble. Hope your feet are up to it."

"My feet are just fine."

As they weaves through the crowd, they met some of their school friends from years past. Many still lived here but some had come home to Fagan just for the celebration and the chance to get together again with old chums. Bert bought a couple of rye and cokes from the liquor booth for Angeline and himself and when he returned, found her chatting to an attractive but plump woman he didn't recognize.

The woman laughed, her eyes crinkling at the corners. "He doesn't remember me, Angie!"

"Oh, sure he does! Bert, you remember Sally Hickert, don't you? She and her brother Ted are a little younger than us. They started school when you were in your last year."

He didn't remember the face but found it pleasant. "Oh, something is familiar about that smile."

She laughed. "I was just a little thing back then, you probably didn't even notice me. But I remember you! My, you were a handsome devil!"

Bert laughed and dropped his eyes. He felt his face flush with embarrassment. Had it been that long since a woman had found him attractive?

Angeline laughed. "Don't believe for a minute that he's shy, Sally. This is one stubborn man standing before you."

Bert glared at his sister. Sally chuckled and grabbed his arm. "Well, he's still handsome."

Angeline said, "Bert, why don't you have a dance with Sally? I see someone over there I'd like to say hello to."

"My pleasure—if you'd like to, Sally," he said, the rum warming his veins. She was a willing and energetic dance partner. They danced a waltz or two while she told him she had two grown daughters, had been married and divorced, but was now single and ready to try again. Bert nodded pleasantly, enjoying the feel of her bouncing flesh but not listening to her chatter. Then he noticed, off to the side, Pearl and Simon, talking to a couple he didn't recognize.

The next dance was a lively polka. Bert spun Sally around to the music, until they were both out of breath.

"I must stop for a while. You don't mind, do you Bert?" Sally panted.

"Not at all, I'm winded myself." She excused herself to go find a lady's room. Bert slipped away to the liquor booth.

He bought a few extra rum tickets, drinking one quickly before getting another. A mixture of elation and dread churned inside of him, seeing Pearl there with Simon. He stood not far away, off to the side where they couldn't see him, and watched.

Simon had grown fat over the years. His thick black moustache gave him the appearance of a walrus, an image enhanced by his aggressive voice. He was loud above the others, likely from too much drinking. His hand waved in the air as he spoke, and the liquid sloshed over the edge of the glass. Pearl stood back from him so he wouldn't slop beer on her. She wore a pink flowered dress that clung to her figure; he inhaled deeply when he looked at her.

"Bert!" Sally had found him.

"There you are," he said. Did you want to go for another spin?"

"Sure."

They danced in the crowd of happy revellers. Angeline had found a dance partner and seemed to be having a wonderful time. It pleased Bert to see her enjoying herself. He kept her in sight, and when she and her partner finished dancing, he told Sally he needed to have a rest. He left the woman with Angeline.

Bert sought out Pearl in the din of the crowd, now boisterous and in high spirits. He first saw Simon, passed out on a bench in front of the grocery store with a couple of his drinking buddies beside him. Pearl was standing beside her drunken husband. She looked embarrassed. Angeline was having a good time; she and Chuck Webster were kicking up their heels to the music with vigour. He didn't see Sally anywhere.

Pearl made her way to the liquor booth and Bert followed her. She ordered a ginger ale. Bert smoothed his hair and, after checking that Simon was asleep, walked over to Pearl. She saw him coming and smiled when he approached.

"Hello, Bert."

"Pearl."

The years between the past and present melted away—a distant dream, seeming to belong to someone else. They were meeting again as two new people.

She glanced around the noisy party. "It's been a long time since we've seen a celebration like this around here!"

"That's for sure," he replied. Her skin was shiny and pink, though it may have been from the rouge, and her hair held its rich, auburn colour. Her face had become wrinkled but she was still beautiful, he thought, and those green eyes still shone. The rye he had been drinking had lowered his resistance to her presence. She seemed to be enjoying herself, and the effect she had upon him

"It's so nice to see you again. I haven't seen you since . . . since Peter's funeral."

Bert remained unfettered. He didn't want to talk about it. For the first time in many years, he had the chance to be somewhat alone with her. He didn't want to waste one moment.

"It's been a long time." His kind, ageing eyes gleamed. "Would you care to dance, madame?" he said, with a deep bow.

She nodded her head, and her eyes became wet as she laughed. "Why, of course, sir!"

He took her hand and they wove through the crowded street to the centre of the festivity. They danced and laughed, and Bert spun her gently as they moved to the songs they remembered from their youth. Bert glanced now and again to ensure Simon still slumped on the bench in a drunken sleep. The air was hot from the summer, and bodies crowded around them while they tried to catch their breath between songs. The band played *The Traitor's Waltz*, and Pearl remarked that she loved that song.

"I remember," he replied softly, pulling her to him.

He closed his eyes as they danced. One or two heads turned, including Sally's, when they noticed Pearl Whiteman dancing very close to Bert McCarthy, but neither of them seemed to notice or care. At the end of the waltz, Bert felt his head spinning from the heat and the rum. He looked into her face and saw the girl he loved so many years ago. Pearl slipped her arms around his waist and kissed him. When they parted, her eyes darted around them to see if anyone had noticed.

"Oh Bertie, I'm still married."

The spell that had hypnotized Bert was broken. They looked over at Simon, a round lump in the corner that was arousing laughter from the people around him.

"I haven't forgotten."

He took her elbow and led her out of the crowd, away from the music. He noticed that Simon was beginning to move. The burden of reality was sinking down upon them.

"I've got to go, Bert. Simon will see us."

"Well, go then," he replied. Was she always to be a source of torture? he wondered. She tried to find his eyes, but he wouldn't look at her. Time had seemed to harden him. He turned away from her.

"Goodbye, Pearl. Nice seeing you."

Pearl watched his back as he walked away. Then she scurried to her husband. Simon regained a groggy awareness of his surroundings, slurring his words so loudly that Bert could hear him above the crowd. It wasn't long before Pearl shuffled him away from the festivity.

Angeline had a hangover the next day. When she came downstairs, she teased Bert that some of the old gang noticed him dancing with Pearl. "Especially Sally," she chided. "She was heart-broken that you didn't come back to ask her for the last dance of the night."

He became surly and she shrugged, giving up on conversation. She poured herself a tall glass of tomato juice and carried it back upstairs to bed. Bert tended to their mother that day.

Mrs. McCarthy passed away at the age of ninety-two. Though caring for her in recent years had been difficult for

Angeline and Bert, her presence was missed. Angeline herself had not aged well. She had become weak and was often sick. Bert's health seemed steady and his eyes were sharp, though his once strong body was now stiff, and his heartbeats were somewhat irregular at times.

Gerald, Pearl's grandson, grew to be a tall young man with orange-red hair. He attended the University of Toronto after high school and earned a degree in Business Administration. Gerald found a job with an electronics company in the city, and in 1975 he married a city girl. Catherine told them her name was Debra and that they had two little girls.

Simon died the year the second child was born. Apparently his drinking had eventually caught up with him. He succumbed to cirrhosis of the liver after dropping in weight to 110 pounds, Catherine said—difficult to envision considering his size before he became ill.

When Bert heard that Simon had died, he had no intention of going to the funeral, or even the parlour. But during the time Simon was laid out at MacDuff's Funeral Home, Angeline had become stricken by a strong bout of the flu. Bert worried that it might be too much for her. He drove Angeline to her doctor in town.

"Damn doctors don't make house calls anymore," he grumbled. He led her into the office, practically carrying her as she leaned on his arm. After a long wait, they called her in to see him.

Bert slipped out to the hardware store to buy some nails. It was on his way back that he saw Pearl walking up the street toward him. She was dressed in black. Her old woman's body still looked trim and elegant, though her steps were shorter than he remembered.

"My condolences, Pearl," he said in a starched voice. His eyebrows met in a scowl when he realized the coldness in his voice, but he couldn't stop it.

"Thank you, Bertie." Her skin looked papery and fragile, and the once auburn hair had turned snowy white. He was shocked by the drastic change, and wondered if it had been dyed the last time he had seen her. She was pretty, though. He saw the small white teeth were still her own when she parted her unpainted, pink lips. They stood there, awkward in the moment. Why had she called him Bertie? He wanted to run in the opposite direction if his old legs would let him but he stayed there, gazing across the street. Pearl touched his arm and gave it a gentle squeeze.

Bert unfurrowed his brows and stared at her. He touched the small dry hand that rested on his arm and patted it. He remembered all the other times that same hand had touched him: as children, as lovers, at dances, in love, in joy, in misery. There was not much more he could feel, or experience, with Pearl.

"I'd best be going."

He didn't look at her again. Pearl stood and watched him leave, watched him walk away from her. After a few moments, she turned and headed toward the funeral home.

Bert went the opposite direction, sweat breaking upon his forehead. He wanted to turn around and grab her and kiss her, but his common sense kept his feet pounding the sidewalk toward the doctor's office.

"Another man's widow!" he huffed, trying to control the emotions churning inside him. He clutched his chest and upon reaching the waiting room, collapsed into a chair. His breaths were strong and short. It took several minutes for him to relax and for the pain in his chest to ebb.

Angeline came out of one of the rooms, barely able to walk. Bert rose from his seat and helped her out the door. In her poor health she didn't notice the disturbed, pale appearance of her brother's face. On the way home, Bert, oblivious to his sister, was consumed with thoughts of Pearl. He wondered how long she would torment his life.

Angeline didn't regain her strength after that bout of the flu. She remained in a weakened condition, and every cold or sickness dragged her further down. In the cool spring of 1982, she contracted pneumonia after staying outside on the porch too long. Bert had tried to get her to come indoors sooner but she refused; she was enjoying the sunshine too much.

They took her by ambulance to the hospital a few days later. Bert thought she might recover, but within two weeks Angeline was gone.

Bert missed her gentle humour and companionship. Not just a sister, she had been his loyal friend throughout the years. Catherine visited occasionally, but her incessant prattle got on his nerves. She did, though, always have some tidbit of information to share about the Varsey's. He learned that Edward still ran the Varsey farm, though he had to hire a fellow a while back to look after it. He and Pearl lived there alone after Simon's death. Apparently, Pearl told everyone that she lived for the times when Gerald and his family visited from the city.

Bert stayed alone at the farm. He hadn't been able to work it himself for the past twelve years. First he had that leg injury in 1973; then the heart problems took hold of him.

He couldn't afford to hire anyone, so he rented the land to his neighbour, Henry Schwaab, a nephew of Matt's wife, Katie. He still tended the garden, and the poultry provided eggs and meat. The hardest part was selling off the cattle. They had made a good milking herd.

He invested the money in a small annuity at the bank's recommendation. With the income he received for renting the land and his pension, there was enough money for him to get by. Now his days passed with a predictability he found reassuring.

As he was eating his cereal, Bert watched the Schwaab boys toss the last hay bales on top of the teetering load. They moved with such ease and strength, and their brown bodies shone with sweat. It had been a long time since he had been able to do that kind of work. They drove the tractor with its full load past his window and out the lane to their farm next door. They waved at Bert, but he just stared back at them. They'd be coming back for another load in awhile; no point in waving, he thought.

He sat back down in his rocker and picked up the paper, again reading the notice: *Peacefully, in her home . . .*

Now Pearl was dead.

Part 3

Bert rubbed his grizzled face with shaky, withered hands. "Won't be long and I'll be joining you all," he muttered as he rocked back and forth in the chair. He sat steeped in memories—unconscious of the Schwaab boys driving in and out his lane—until the sun went down. He went to sleep easily that night, exhausted from his imaginary journey back in time, weary from reliving the events of his life.

Bert arose the next morning at the same time as any other day, determined to maintain order in his existence. After breakfast he worked in the garden, picking the second crop of beans that were ripe and ready for collecting. He didn't bother with his afternoon nap but spent the day cutting the beans, blanching and preparing them for freezing. He wouldn't let his sentimental recollections destroy another day.

Barely a month later at the kitchen table, after a dinner of pork and beans, another ad in the Herald caught his eye. He read it under Auction Sales:

Estate Sale of Pearl Whiteman. July 21 at 11 o'clock. Rain or shine. Two miles east on Concession 4 off of the Sixth Line, out of Paisley. Household effects, farm machinery, antiques in excellent condition.

Item by item, Bert read through the list. The antiques were at the end:

... spinning wheel, two butter churns, antique china, washstand, old shotgun, gingerbread clock, La Favourite gramophone with records ...

Bert dropped the paper in his lap. She had kept the gramophone after all these years. He picked up the paper and continued:

... maple-spooled settee, Victorian sofa, rocking chair. Don't miss this sale!

He threw the paper on the kitchen table. "She's barely dead and they're selling her things. Vultures!" Where was Edward, the weasel? he wondered, thinking he must be the one doing this. Bert sighed, picked up the empty pot and spoon he used for his dinner and threw them in the sink.

That evening on the porch, he wondered about his own death and how it would be for him. He wished it would happen right there on the farm, on a summer day. Hopefully, he would know when it was coming. He would go into the fields and sit down on the earth. He would run his fingers through the soil. Then death could take him. Then they could rummage through his things, like they would Pearl's, and the rich people from the city could come up and take it all away. The bitterness that swaddled him fell away, loosened by the realization of his mortality.

Bert thought about the gramophone as the sun cast its warm glow across the green fields of freshly cut hay. It reminded him of the time in the Varsey parlour so many years ago, when he and Pearl had danced together and held each other close. He could almost hear the music.

"Damn! I'm going to get that gramophone," he sputtered through his toothless gums. He limped into the house and dug through the kitchen drawer, searching through the bills. His old hands drew out his bank book and he flipped through the pages. He had four hundred and fifty dollars in his account that he had been saving for a rainy day. It took him three years to collect it from what little he could spare from his pension cheques. Surely no one would bid higher than that! He chuckled to himself, stuffing the bank book in his pocket.

The next day Bert drove to the bank. The teller cast a strange look at the old man demanding all of the money from his account.

"Are you sure this is what you want to do," she said.

"Yes! It's my money and I want it now," he argued.

"Fine, sir." She reluctantly gave him the cash and he huffed, snatching it from her hands. She worried about an old man carrying that much money.

Bert rolled up the bills and stashed them in his hip pocket. He stomped out of the bank. On the way home, he fumed. "Just because I'm old, they think my brain's gone to pulp!"

The day of the sale began muggy and still, but a cool breeze soon relieved the heat. "Gonna be a scorcher," he said.

Bert gazed through the opened bedroom curtain at the fields below. He never tired of the sight.

He searched through the boxes of summer clothes piled in one of the upstairs bedrooms until he pulled out a white nylon shirt and a pair of navy blue trousers he hadn't seen in years. Silly, he thought; he felt like he was going to see Pearl. Old fool! he chastised.

Bert cooked the cereal and finished his breakfast, cleaned his dentures, and pushed them onto his sore and tender gums. He grabbed his old straw hat as he went out the door and limped outside to the old truck. It started immediately. He put it into gear and drove to the Varsey farm at a slow, steady speed.

His heart began to pound when he arrived at their laneway. He remembered parking his bicycle there the last time he had visited on that drizzly night a lifetime before. To think he hadn't been here in almost sixty years! He turned into the lane. The huge yellow house still looked ominous and grand. Though the wood trim needed painting, it looked like Pearl and Edward had kept the place in good repair.

There must have been twenty cars there already, and the auction wasn't to start for another hour. He noticed a young man in an orange vest waving furiously at him. Bert turned the truck to the right and parked by the barn doors.

He got out of the vehicle with difficulty and stretched his legs. He wanted to slip into the barn to see the inside of it again, but there were several signs posted outside that read "No Admittance". He noted the old milk house had been torn down, and there was an addition to the barn. Through the large window he observed the huge milk cooler that stood inside and he felt a sting of envy. Bert had never been able to afford anything quite so modern for his farm. His animals were sold before that type of milk cooler was even made. He suddenly felt very old and tired.

He left the barn and walked past the farm machinery and garden tools. In front of the house, dozens of people buzzed about on the front lawn, handling the items that were neatly placed upon the tables. He walked past the dishes and pots, not recognizing anything. He had never actually been invited into the Varsey home, except by Pearl. He continued past the furniture. There were a few beds and dressers and a fashionable green couch and chairs.

Bert came upon the antique furniture. He saw the black lacquer chairs that had impressed him in his youth. Next to them was the gold velvet Victorian sofa that he and Pearl had sat on during their clandestine meetings, and where Bert had stolen a kiss or two. He smiled as he reminisced.

Another set of tables was lined behind the furniture. The antiques were set upon white linen table cloths. There was some gold-edged china that Angeline would have loved, an old shotgun that probably belonged to old man Varsey, and the gingerbread clock that was now silent. Bert remembered how the tick-tock would fill the parlour when the music stopped. At the end of the table he saw the gramophone.

He limped over to it and rubbed his hands over the fine oak cabinet. He opened the lid and read *La Favourite*. It looked the same as it did back in 1927. Bert wound the handle on the right side; the springs still seemed to be working. He opened the front doors of the cabinet. There were about a dozen records inside, and a box on the ground beside it was full of 78's. He crouched, careful not to fall over, and examined the records one by one until he read a label he recognized. Bert pulled out *The Traitor's Waltz.* He gently placed in on the round disc, cranked the handle, and lowered the needle.

The familiar crinkling noise came through the speaker, and Bert adjusted the volume. Sweet, slow music drifted out through the wooden lattice. Bert stood and listened, eyes closed, rocking slightly to the music. Pearl was there with him as they bobbed and swayed; she laughed and threw back her head, and he kissed her. When the music stopped, he opened his eyes and lifted the needle from the record. He noticed a small boy looking up at him.

"How old are you, mister?"

His eyes crinkled against the morning sunlight. Bert put the record back in the cabinet.

"Well?"

"Why?"

"Because I've never seen anyone as old as you," he replied with sincerity.

Bert laughed at the candour of childhood, and his teeth clacked. "Seventy-seven."

"Wow!"

Soon a young couple rushed to the boy. They ignored Bert as if he wasn't there.

"There you are!" The woman in the red sun-dress and matching hat screeched at the child. "Tristan, how many times have we told you not to run away like that! Oh look, Barry! What a darling old Victrola!"

Her husband, wearing dark sunglasses, examined the machine. He was a vision in matching white shirt and shorts. A yellow sweater hung around his neck, deliberate and casual, despite the heat. "Mmm." He flipped through the records in the box.

"Let's get it, hon!"

"Whatever for, Tina?"

He glanced after his son who had run off to the next table and was staring at a woman with her foot in a cast.

"I think it would look absolutely adorable in that drab corner in the family room. I've been wondering what to put there; this would be perfect."

"Gee, Teen. I was hoping for something a little more *mo-derne,* " he griped.

"But Barry, think of the fun it would be at parties! Everyone would get a charge out of it."

"Mmm. I suppose we could turn it into a liquor cabinet," he added as they walked to the next table.

Bert's eyes followed them. City folk, just like he figured. He turned back to the gramophone and placed another record on the turntable. This time he put on Wilf Carter's *Wreck of the Forty-Nine.* When the music started, he tapped his foot to the rhythm and saw Pearl clapping her hands and twirling before him. When the song ended, he played *Doin' What Comes Naturally.* He had visions of his brother Joseph singing the song, just as he did the day he left to enlist in the army. He laughed aloud, remembering the humorous way Joseph contorted his face when he mimicked the song. A raspy voice behind Bert startled him.

"Well, Bert McCarthy! I thought it was you over here."

He turned around and saw Edward Varsey standing behind him. He was still short and round, Bert thought, and his eyes still small and squinty.

"Edward." Bert lifted the needle of the gramophone and removed the record.

"I should have known by the music it was you," Edward chuckled. Bert felt his face getting warm. "Oh, don't get sore at me. I just meant that Pearl told me you always liked the gramophone."

Bert softened. "She did?"

"Sure." Edward laughed again. There was something in the sound that was reminiscent of Pearl. Edward became solemn. "I'm sure going to miss her. But I guess it's a blessing she went the way she did." Bert looked at him, puzzled. "She had cancer, you know. Had it for years, but she never said much about it. She died in her sleep, poor soul. I guess we all have to go, and by God it's as good a way to go as any." Bert glared at him and wondered how he could be so callous. He never did like Edward much. "So, are you going to bid on this old thing?"

Bert hesitated before nodding.

"Well, I hope you get it. Pearl would have wanted you to have it." Bert was surprised by the kindness. "You know Bert," Edward continued in a hushed voice, "I knew all about it."

Bert's eyes bulged and he stared at Edward, speechless. "I knew she cared for you, way back when we were kids. You should have seen the beating she took from the old man when he found out you tried to visit her that rainy night. She defended you and your family, and she told him she loved you. But he wouldn't listen. Miserable bastard."

He paused for a moment's reflection.

"He let her have it with the belt. It woke us all up. Us kids, we were just shaking. He pushed that wedding to Simon so fast it would make your head spin—anything to keep the farm."

Bert's mind was swimming with pictures of Pearl: of himself as a young man, of the two of them together, of the night they made love, of Edward's beady eyes as he teased them, of the day Matt told him she was going to marry another man . . . he took a few deep breaths to calm himself.

"I didn't know."

"I didn't think so. That's why I took your bike home that day. I thought you should have been told, just in case you wanted to take her away with you. I loved her too, you know, even though we had our disagreements as kids. I really think she would have gone with you. And, I guess there was a romantic part of me somewhere that thought the two of you were meant to be together. You were so sick in bed they couldn't even wake you up. Are you alright?"

Bert clutched his chest and Edward helped him to one of the old black chairs. "I'm fine," he wheezed. "Just have to catch my breath, that's all."

"Sure hope so. Anyhow, I was sure surprised to find out you had pneumonia when I got to your place. Your mother was a very nice lady, wasn't she, Bert? She had me in for lemonade and I told her all about everything. She was sure worried about you." Edward looked away for a moment. "Pearl and I got really close these past few years, ever since Simon died, the old lush. She didn't have much of a life with him, not after Peter died. Simon just couldn't handle it. Thank the Lord she had Gerald to look after; gave her a reason to live, she said. He and his family are here today, you know. They're running the sale."

Bert rubbed his chin and looked at Edward with mixed emotions. After years of intense dislike for Edward, he now felt gratitude and appreciation. This was a side of Edward he never knew existed. But then again, Bert had never made any effort to get to know him as an adult. For the first time, he wondered about Edward's future. He couldn't have had an easy life either. They shared the common history of farm people—hard work and love of the land. "What are you going to do, Edward?"

"Me? Why, I'm moving into town. Gerald's got me a nice apartment in Sunnyhaven. It's just for seniors, you know. I've had enough of the old place. We've listed it with an agent out of Fagan. They're supposed to be pretty good. You should sell your place, Bert."

"No."

"I know, I know. You'll be there till you drop." He chuckled. "See? I know you better than you think." He winked. "Well, I better make sure nobody's walking off with the cutlery. Good luck with the gramophone. By the way, keep your eye on that lady over there." He pointed to an attractive blonde woman in her early forties. Her hair was tied back with a pink chiffon scarf. "She's an antique dealer up from the city. Friend of Gerald's. She goes to lots of auctions, buying up antiques for her business down in Markham. Her name's Marion Poole. Well, I'll see you later." With a small wave he jaunted over to the household goods.

Bert tried to absorb everything that Edward had said. If he hadn't been so foolish that night in the rain and gotten himself sick—if he had gone straight home instead—would Pearl have run away with him? It was too much to consider now, there on the front lawn of the Varsey farm, surrounded by the things that Pearl had loved and lived with until her death. He pushed the thought from his mind and made his way to the hay mower where there were a few shade trees and not so many people.

Bert soon heard the auctioneer calling out on the microphone, asking for everyone to come up to the house. The auction was about to start. By this time, there were about sixty people at the sale, and still more cars were pulling into the laneway.

The household contents were sold first. Bert stood back in the shade and wiped his forehead, waiting for the auctioneer to get to the antiques. It seemed to take a long time, but there were many small items on the tables still to be auctioned. It was an hour before they reached the living room suite. Bert ambled closer when they finally arrived at the antique furniture.

He listened to the bidding. Four, five, six hundred finally bought the Victorian sofa from the parlour. A crisp-looking woman in her sixties bought it, "For the Cardin County Museum in Walston," Bert heard her tell an inquisitive onlooker. He was pleased that it would be preserved for posterity. It made him feel somewhat immortal. People would see the sofa that he and Pearl shared—one that held many memories—for years after he was gone.

The bidding continued, and the crowd seemed frantic to buy. Marion Poole had been eyeing the gingerbread clock. Once the bidding started, she calmly nodded past three hundred, three fifty, three seventy-five—

"Sold! To the lovely lady in the pink scarf," the auctioneer barked.

A tight smile crossed her lips and she nodded to a young man behind her. He picked it up and set it aside with the assortment of other items she had so far collected. She remained in her place in front of the auctioneer.

A small, maple spinning wheel was auctioned next. Bert wondered if Mrs. Varsey was the one who had used it. He had never known Pearl to spin as far as he could remember. He heard a familiar shrill voice beside him: "Oh Barry, I've got to have that spinning wheel! It would look so cute upstairs on the landing!" The woman in the red dress again, he thought, remembering her name was Tina. He watched them bid.

"One hundred!" Tina began the bidding with a toothy smile, and her husband grinned casually beside her. One fifty was the bid from Marion Poole who she shot an icy glance at Tina. Two hundred! Two fifty, two seventy-five, three hundred—

"Three fifty!" shouted Tina. She cast a haughty leer at Marion Poole who then rolled her eyes and continued bidding.

"Three seventy-five, three-eighty, four hundred! Once, twice, sold! Again to the pretty lady in pink!" The auctioneer droned on, playing the mood of his audience like a violin. Tina pouted; her husband flung an arm around her, all the while maintaining his static grin.

Bert wiped the sweat from his face. The bidding was much higher than he had anticipated, and wondered about his chances of getting the gramophone. Marion Poole had moved over in front of it and was waiting for the auctioneer to finish with the table. Bert sidled to the end of the table and positioned himself where he would be sure to get the auctioneer's attention, yet far back enough to watch his competition.

Eventually the mob reached the gramophone.

Tina was smiling broadly and chewing gum, and Bert could hear her shrill yapping above the din of the crowd. He took a deep breath and again wiped his face. The sun was beating down on him where he stood. It will all be over soon, he thought.

The auctioneer cooed and awed over "the fine piece of antiquity" that stood before him, and "the impeccable condition" of the gramophone. Bert wished the man would get on with it.

"Where are we going to start the bidding, folks, on this priceless piece of history? Four hundred?"

Bert's eyes widened; he was afraid he would lose before it even started. The lady from the museum slowly lifted her hand and said, "Two hundred".

They were off.

"Two hundred, do I hear two fifty? Two fifty, give me three hundred? Three hundred, how about three fifty? Three fifty?" The bidding had slowed enough for Bert to raise his hand for his first bid. The lady from the museum dropped out. Marion Poole was one of the three bidders now left, but he didn't see the other one.

"Three seventy-five!" a voice squeaked to the left of him. It was Tina.

"Four hundred, do I have four hundred?"

Marion Poole hesitated a few seconds, then nodded.

"Four twenty-five, do I have four twenty-five, folks?" Bert raised his hand. He could see Edward behind the auctioneer, watching with his intense little eyes.

"Four fifty, do I have four fifty?"

Marion Poole shook her head and walked away. "It's not worth that," she said to the young man with her as she left the crowd.

"Four fifty!" Tina screeched, and she jiggled up and down beside her ever-grinning husband.

He only had four hundred and fifty dollars in his pocket. Bert felt the wad of money. He figured he had almost a hundred more in his chequing account. His next pension cheque wasn't due for three more weeks. The auctioneer stared at him.

"Do I hear four seventy-five? Four seventy-five? Anyone?" He searched the crowd with his eyes. "She's a beauty, folks. Lots of 78's with her too."

"Here!" Bert called out, shaking his fist in the air.

"Five hundred!" Tina's wide mouth spat.

Her husband put his arm around her and his other hand in his pocket. He was still grinning. "Gotta have it, don't you?" he joked, arousing chuckles and attention from the crowd around them. Tina giggled, keeping her eyes focused on the auctioneer. Bert's heart pounded and he breathed deeply.

"Do I hear five twenty-five? Five twenty-five, sir? Five twenty-five?" Bert returned the auctioneer's gaze and he nodded. "We have five twenty-five, folks. Five twenty-five. Anyone for five fifty? Five fifty?"

"Five fifty!" Tina hollered, amidst hoops of laughter around her.

"I have five fifty! Do I have five seventy-five? Five seventy-five?"

Bert looked at the gramophone. He could see Pearl's smiling face as she danced in front of him to *The Traitor's Waltz*, and those green, green eyes.

"Do I have five seventy-five?" The auctioneer stared at him.

Bert shook his head and turned to walk away.

"Only twenty-five more dollars, sir. Five seventy-five. Do I have five seventy-five?"

Bert didn't look back. The crowd watched for his response as he left, and there were a few chuckles. Without turning, he shook his head and waved his arm as if shooing a pesky fly.

"Sold! To the lovely lady in the red hat!"

Bert stopped and watched Tina jumping with joy, hugging her smug husband. "Oooh! It's mine, Barry! I don't believe it!" she wailed.

"I thought it would be when you didn't get that spinning wheel," he added for the benefit of the crowd, and he flashed his white smile.

Bert hobbled toward the truck to leave when Edward called out to him. "Hey, Bert!" He turned around to see Edward puffing as he trotted. "It's too bad you didn't get the gramophone. But don't leave yet, please. There's some folks here I'd like you to meet." He began to walk toward the house; Bert remained standing. "Well, come on! I've just invited you into the Varsey house!" Bert considered it for a moment, and smiled. He followed Edward.

They entered through the screen door. It was new and made of aluminum, but the inside of the summer kitchen looked the same—even the solid door to the house that was shut in his face the last time he was there. Edward opened the kitchen door for him, and Bert removed his hat and stepped inside. A petite, plain-looking young woman was making sandwiches for two little girls that sat at the table.

"Hello," the woman said. Her cheeks dimpled.

"Bert, I'd like you to meet Debra, Gerald's wife. And these two little darlings are their children. This is Carrie, and this here is Lisa."

Debra nodded, and the girls stared at their sandwiches. Carrie, the oldest with brown hair, spoke. "Hello."

"Hello there," Bert replied. The child's attention went back to her lunch.

Edward led Bert to a chair and sat beside him at the far end of the long table. Bert watched the young faces. Carrie's eyes were green, like Pearl's. Lisa was blonde with big, blue eyes. Both girls seemed very tiny. Bert figured they got that from their mother.

Edward said, "Mr. McCarthy here used to know your great grandmother."

"You knew gramma?" Carrie's eyes opened wide, surprising Bert with their sudden interest.

"Yes, I did. I knew her when she was just a girl."

"Holy! What was she like?"

Bert felt a warm glow as he thought of Pearl. Here he sat, at her kitchen table, with their great grandchildren. What a strange way the world works, he thought. Edward watched him, his small eyes wet. Bert smiled at the children, feeling more alive than he had in years.

"Well, Miss Pearl Varsey was the prettiest girl that I ever saw." The girls sat transfixed, listening to the stranger that knew gramma. "She had long auburn hair that hung down around her shoulders, and big green eyes that shone when she smiled. Just like yours," he said to Carrie, and she blushed. Lisa giggled. He looked at the younger child. "And she had a laugh just like yours. It made you feel very happy when she laughed."

"I know! Gramma liked to have fun!" Lisa took a bite of her sandwich.

"She was a kind woman," Bert concluded.

"I miss her," Carrie said. Bert nodded softly.

"We all miss her, dear," Debra said. "But she's happy in heaven now." She smiled at Bert. "Can I get you a cup of tea, Mr. McCarthy?"

"No, thank you. I've got to get going. But thank you," he repeated, struggling to his feet.

Edward followed him to the door. Bert turned to the mother and her children.

"It was a pleasure to meet you," he said with an air of gallantry as he held his straw hat to his stomach.

"Well, it was nice meeting you too."

Carrie said, "Goodbye, mister!" Lisa echoed her. Bert waved at them as he left.

"Aren't they little dolls?" Edward asked when they were on the porch. "Pearl adored them. They were everything to her these past few years."

A tall, red-headed fellow strode up the walk toward them. Edward's eyes lit up. "There he is!" The young man gave Edward a brisk bear hug. "Gerald, you'll never guess who this is. Bert McCarthy!"

Bert felt ill at ease and he stared at the ground.

Gerald extended his hand. "Hello, Mr. McCarthy," he said. Respect radiated from his voice.

Bert beheld the handsome young man. So this is my grandson, he thought. He saw the resemblance to himself as a youth in the structure of his face and nose, and in his smile. "Just call me Bert. Please."

Gerald smiled. "Hello, Bert." Edward enjoyed observing the encounter. "I'm so glad to meet you, sir. Ma—gramma Pearl—told me about you after Grandfather Simon died." Bert shuffled where he stood, and felt his neck getting warm. He didn't know just what Gerald knew of him. "She cared about you very much. You must have been very special to her," Gerald continued. "It's so nice to meet someone who was close to her. She was the only mother I ever knew."

Bert cleared his throat. "I'm glad I met you, too. I'm sure you made Pearl's life very happy."

They stood on the veranda and looked at each other, not speaking. Bert took Gerald's hand in his and squeezed it.

"Yes, it has been so good to meet you, son."

They heard the auctioneer shout, "Sold!" and the crowd in the yard hummed in excitement. Gerald surveyed the swarm making its way to the barn. "Well, I better get some lunch. The sale turned out to be much bigger than we expected." He smiled. "See you, Bert."

"See you," he replied. Bert called after him, "You have a very nice family."

"Thanks." Gerald disappeared into the house.

Bert adjusted his hat. "I'd better be on my way. It won't be easy getting out of here with all these cars everywhere." He turned his attention to Edward. "Thank you."

Edward wiped his eyes. "For what? I didn't do anything."

"Yes, you did. More than you know."

The two old men smiled at each other. "Why don't you visit me at Sunnyhaven sometime, Bert? I'll be there within the month. We can have a game of checkers."

"I'll do that," Bert replied, as he descended the stairs. "And when you feel the need for country air, stop by the farm. Bring Gerald and his family, will you?"

"You bet I will."

Bert limped to his truck, unaware of the crowd that had gathered around the auctioneer at the hay mower.

Acknowledgements

In the past century, the demographic trend in Ontario shifted away from rural living on the family farm to urban life in larger centres. I wish to thank my parents and Laura and Charles for sharing these experiences and those passed on to them by their ancestors during those transitional times.

I would also like to thank my mother for loaning her archival photographs used to enhance the cover of this book.

The characters in this story are fictional; the world they lived in was not.